A Passionate Night

Candace Shaw

Blurb

Mixing business with pleasure leads to a passionate night.

Harper Bennett's motto is work hard, play hard. Lately, she's forgotten the latter and has focused her time as part-owner, along with her brothers, of the hottest nightclub in Atlanta. When an intriguing client enters, Harper forgoes her promise to never date a man that doesn't live in the same city and she finds herself playing hard to get with Hunter Arrington. The passion that has ignited between them can't be extinguished, and she dreads the day he has to leave.

Hunter travels the world because of his career and has no intentions of settling down until his eyes land on Harper Bennett. There's something about the petite, sassy woman that he adores and makes him feel at home for the first time in years. Now he's faced with a life-changing decision and the thought of being without Harper isn't an option.

Chapter One

"Please, and I do mean *please* as your job depends on this ... make sure that you keep the bottles flowing and Unique along with his crew overly happy," Harper Bennett demanded to the waitress, as she sashayed down the hall of VIP rooms before pushing the door leading to the mezzanine level open. Her inquisitive eyes scanned the floors and sitting areas to make sure the cleaning crew had been thorough that morning. Satisfied, the ladies headed toward the escalator to travel down to the main floor.

"I'll have everything set up in the all-white VIP room according to his rider. He was furious with the last club that didn't and blasted them all over social media. Club Masquerade is the hottest club in Atlanta and we intend to keep it that way. Humph, he should've booked his party here in the first place like all of his other fellow rapper buddies."

"Yes, Ms. Bennett," Dawn replied, nodding her head as the ladies stepped onto the escalator together.

Harper checked her to-do list for the rest of the day on her iPad and scrunched her forehead at the last minute meeting her assistant had set up. The one that started in ten minutes. Placing her focus back on the important situation at hand, she looked her top VIP cocktail waitress square in the eye. Yes, she trusted Dawn like she trusted herself, but Harper still needed to get her point across. "Don't make him regret having his birthday celebration here, or *me* for selecting you to be his personal waitress. Windi and Joslyn will assist you. Thank you for coming in on your off day but be back at eight sharp."

Dismissing Dawn, Harper stepped off the elevator and continued into the main area of the club as her black Jimmy Choo's clicked against the empty wood dance floor—which in a couple of hours would be packed with people dancing to the latest hip hop and pop songs. She spotted two of the bartenders at the huge circular bar sitting in the middle of the club. The men were busy unpacking boxes of liquor that had arrived that afternoon.

"Did you lock the main doors back, Josh?" she asked. Her brother, Mason, hated them being unlocked for an extended period of time when the club was closed.

"Nah. Your assistant said you were expecting a client."

"That's what the call box is for. Next time lock it."

Heading toward the lobby, she turned off her I'm-the-boss-and-don't-you-forget-it persona and switched to the nice and professional event planner that she displayed with potential clients. One of the tinted glass doors of the club opened as the last of the afternoon sun blanketed the area and blinded her for a moment. Squinting, she tried to make out who strolled toward her. The alluring scent of cologne filled her nostrils, and her hand automatically ran through her thick, black tresses that fell to her bra strap.

Geez, I haven't even seen him yet but a man that smells this damn good better look damn good, too.

When the door closed, Harper's lips parted as her eyes feasted on the handsome vision gliding toward her as if he'd stepped off the runway at a fashion show in Paris. Bald? Check. Chocolate? Check. Mouthwatering? Double check. Over six feet tall? Check. The man was scrumptious and his presence outshone the sunlight that he'd shut out.

His medium, muscular-build physique complemented his blue suit, and she had an inkling that his body would complement her as well. Because of her small frame, she preferred a man his size and not an overly built man who would smother her.

He definitely fit the majority of the list minus a deep voice, honest eyes, charming smile, and must be intelligent … which was the deal breaker. Nothing else mattered if he didn't have a brain. When he slid his shades off not only were his eyes honest they were also a mesmerizing light brown. An electric force jolted through Harper's body, and her stomach tightened when he ran a sensual gaze over her pink halter blouse and black pencil skirt. The heat radiating from him soared through her, causing heated goose bumps to cascade down her arm. A charming, sexy smile raised the left side of his face, and the stifled sigh in her windpipe managed to escape anyway. Check. Check.

Okay, stop acting like you've never seen a handsome man before! Now to see if his voice meets the criteria.

"Welcome to Club Masquerade. May I help you?" she asked in a steady, professional tone and was relieved when the frog in her throat didn't leap off its lily pad. The man was undeniably gorgeous, and she silently chastised herself for becoming unraveled right in front of him. Perhaps he wouldn't notice.

"Yes. I'm Hunter Arrington. I'm here to meet with Harper Bennett," he answered in a deep, penetrating voice. "Do you know if he's available?"

As Harper processed what he'd asked, and made a mental check on her list next to deep voice along with extra points for making her tremble, she realized he was her appointment. *Dang it.* She never mixed business with pleasure. But at least he would be eye candy for the next hour … maybe two if she spoke really, *really* slow.

Placing her professional cap on with super glue, she smiled pleasantly and held out her right hand. "I *am* Harper Bennett, Mr. Arrington."

Wrinkling his forehead, a surprised grin appeared on Hunter's delectable lips as he slid her hand in his. "Forgive me, Ms. Bennett. I was under the impression that you were a man because of your first name. My assistant made the appointment, but um …" He paused his embarrassed ramble, squeezing her hand and flashing a sinfully suave smile. "But goodness was I wrong."

Reluctantly sliding her hand away from his warm, caressing one—because it was way too comfortable intermingled with hers—she stepped back a tad and hoped he didn't hear the fast, off-beat of her heart throbbing hard against her chest. "No problem. I know my name is somewhat unisex. My parents thought I was going to be a boy and Harper is my mother's maiden name. So they still decided to use it."

"They didn't see on the sonogram that you were a girl? Or did they want to be surprised?"

"No. There were two other babies with me," she explained. "I'm the youngest of triplets."

He attempted to suppress a naughty smirk, but he didn't succeed and instead stepped closer to her. "So there's three of you?" The devilish grin emerged even wider as he tapped his chin. "Damn."

Harper noted the gulp on his Adam's apple and the curious raise of his eyebrow as she could only imagine what dirty fantasy he'd conjured up in his brain with triplets who were identical to her. She shook her head. "No. Not exactly. I'm the only girl. I have two older-by-a-few-minutes, overprotective brothers." She held in a laugh when his wicked smile quickly faded.

Clearing his throat, Hunter simply nodded and slid his hands into his suit slacks. "Oh, I see. Cool. I have a twin brother."

Now the fantasy jumped into her brain as a grin that matched his from earlier arose. "Soooooooo, there really are two of you? Uh huh." Pressing her lips, she tapped her chin.

4

"Um … we're fraternal twins but we look similar. Same complexion, bald head, height, and build, but different personalities and interests. He's my best friend, though."

"I understand. So are my brothers." Shaking her head to clear it of the amorous thoughts clouding it, she remembered why they were standing there in the first place. "If you want to follow me, we can go ahead and discuss your fundraiser."

He chuckled. "Yeah, I almost forgot why I was here."

After relocking the doors, Harper led him to one of the oversized booths that sat along the back wall of the club. She slid onto the seat but stayed toward the edge of it. He followed suit on the opposite side and sat directly in front of her. Hunter's long legs stretched out under the table and accidently bumped her outstretched ones. The mere touch sent her pulse racing like a horse aiming to win the Kentucky Derby. Her eyes automatically glanced to the black drapes flanking the booth, which could be closed for privacy. Not that she needed to and was mad her mind even went to that location. Sliding her legs back, she tucked her feet against the bottom of the seat. She couldn't believe the havoc this man caused, and she had to remind herself he was a client.

Opening the note section on her iPad, Harper gave him her attention and prayed her voice wouldn't crack. His smooth, coffee-colored skin was enhanced by the fully lit spotlights that were usually dimmed in an array of colors when the club was open. She had to knock the thought away of how his hand intertwined with her toffee-colored one appeared perfectly together like a tempting swirled mousse pudding with whipped cream and cherries on top.

"So, tell me about your organization and your fundraiser."

"I'm the project director for a non-profit organization, Doctors Unlimited, which specializes in bringing medical care to impoverished places, natural disasters, and epidemic outbreaks. We're mostly outside of the United States but sometimes here as well when needed."

"Oh, yes. I've heard of it." She paused as she remembered his last name. "So wait … you're related to the founder? I've seen him numerous times on the national news outlets discussing the organization." *Guess handsome men run in the Arrington family.*

"Yes, Dr. Cannon Arrington is my cousin. The board has decided to expand to the States now and we're preparing to open a free clinic here in Atlanta and other cities across the US as well. I'm in the States temporarily for the next four months or so to oversee this new venture."

"Oh." The simple word came out in a disappointed fashion, and she had to stop herself from frowning all the while wondering why the heck she cared. She didn't even know the man, yet apart of her wanted to. Nevertheless, it didn't matter because Hunter didn't live in Atlanta. Long distance relationships were no longer on the list after her horrible break-up with an ex she caught cheating two years ago. She'd flown to New York to surprise him for the weekend only to discover a surprise of her own when she found him having sex with some bimbo on the couch.

"Where do you live now?"

"I don't really a have set place where I live. I've been all over the world with the organization for the past twelve years since I graduated from law school. However, Memphis will always be my home. My next assignment after I leave Atlanta is Ghana for about six months. Maybe less. After that who knows? I go where I'm needed."

"Wow. That's truly wonderful. We would love to host your fundraiser gala. I know a lot of bigwigs who would donate to such a caring and prestigious organization. Tell you what, I'll waive half the cost of renting the club if you have it on a Monday evening. That's the only night where we don't have a theme. Unless you'd prefer something during the day when we're closed, but in your case I think a night time event would be fabulous."

"Thank you. I sincerely appreciate it, but you don't need to run that by anyone? A manager? The owner?"

She nearly choked on a laugh. "I *am* the owner along with my two brothers. So no, I don't need to run it by anyone. It will be our donation."

"Forgive me. How did the Bennett triplets get into the nightclub business?"

"Our parents were the original owners for over twenty years. They're retired now and traveling the States in a Winnebago, and sometimes they go abroad. We took over the reins about three years ago. Sometimes my dad still likes to check on things so we humor him. My brother, Cameron, is the general manager, and my brother, Mason, joined us six months ago as head of security after his honorable discharge from the Marines. I've worked here since I graduated from Howard assisting my mother with the event planning."

"That's wonderful. Keeping it all in the family. It's great to see African-American legacies."

"Yes, and it seems you're doing the same."

"Oh, yes. I never wanted to be an attorney like my parents, or a doctor like my cousins, but I've always been one to help people which is pretty much the Arrington family motto. Working with Doctors Unlimited is very fulfilling for me. It's definitely not about the money or accolades. My father came from very humble beginnings, and the one thing my dad and my Uncle Francis instilled in me is never forget where you came from. Always give back. Not just money but your time and concernment for others. That's why opening the free clinics here in the States is very important to me on a personal level."

Something about his statement pulled at her heart strings. If there were such a thing as a perfect man, then he fit the mold. Harper loved a man who had compassion about people and life. There was so much more to him than a dashing smile, ruggedly handsome face, and a chiseled physique. Hunter Arrington possessed the characteristics that she'd searched for. The men she'd dated since her break up were arrogant, haughty rich men who only cared about money and material possessions. Heck, she had her own money—always had—so men thinking that lavishing her with extravagant gifts would impress her were sadly mistaken.

At age thirty-three, Harper wanted so much more from life than the finer things. She wanted the love and stability that her parents had shared for thirty-six years. Hunter was a breath of fresh air and he seemed like a genuine guy, but unfortunately she couldn't find out more. Knowing any more about him would place her in a situation she didn't want to be in.

For the next hour they discussed the details of the event while Harper found herself trying to control the butterflies doing the jitterbug in her stomach. She'd stepped away momentarily to grab two chilled bottled waters from the bar even though she would have preferred a stiff scotch to calm down her attraction to a man she could never date. Hunter was intelligent, articulate, good-looking, and charismatic all wrapped into one. A perfect combination. The more they conversed, the more she craved learning more about him and his experiences that had sent him all over the world because of his caring heart.

"Why did you decide to have the fundraiser at Masquerade?" she asked once they were done with the details, and she sensed he was leaving when he checked his cell phone with a frown. Did he have another appointment? A date?

"One of the volunteers who recently attended an event said it was a very upscale place, and I should consider having the fundraiser here. I've only been in Atlanta for about two months, except when I had to leave briefly for an assignment, and I don't know all of the happening spots. I work all day and afterwards crash in my hotel suite. I haven't had a chance to venture out except for grabbing dinner if I don't order room service."

"Atlanta has a plethora of things to do. You haven't been here before?"

"Yes, but it's usually for work not pleasure."

"Well, you should go out and do something. You work hard and you should play hard. Or at least that's mine and my best friend, London's motto." Even though neither of them were living up to the last part lately.

A sexy grin emerged across his face and he leaned in toward her. "Maybe you can show me some fun places while I'm in town. Be my private tour guide."

Beads of sweat formed on the back of her neck. Was he asking her out on a date? She wanted to say yes—goodness, she wanted to scream yes—but why waste time with a man who didn't even live in Atlanta? "Oh ... um, Hunter ... I don't know if that's such a great idea. I don't mix business with pleasure. You're my client."

"Then I'll find another venue," he stated matter-of-factly.

"You can't do that. You signed a contract," she reminded with a wink.

"Okay ... then it's not a date. Just two grown people hanging out," he paused, resting a heated gaze on her and lowering his voice, "and *playing* hard."

The tremor that raged through her surely had to have shaken the building as well because the intensity in his voice settled right in her center. She crossed and uncrossed her legs while thinking about her next words carefully.

"Can I think about it?" she asked, even though she really wanted to answer, 'Yes and what time are you picking me up?' But she had to remain in control of herself. This wasn't like her at all to be infatuated with a man she'd just met.

An amused expression washed over his features. "Sure. At least you didn't say no."

"Uh … I didn't say yes either. However, why don't you come by the club tomorrow night. We're having our Wind Down Wednesday. We open early at six for happy hour. Drinks and appetizers are half off until eight. Get out and have some fun. You may meet someone." *Wait. Why the hell am I trying to give this masterpiece away?*

A serious grin raised up his left jaw. "I only have my eyes set on you, beautiful one."

Heat rushed to her cheeks as the smile she wanted to suppress burst through followed by a giggle which was so unlike her once again.

"Well, maybe I'll have an answer for you tomorrow evening."

"I hope so." Glancing at his cell phone once more, Hunter stood. "I hate to go, but I have a conference call meeting soon with Cannon and some other members of Doctors Unlimited that are on a different time zone. It's almost nine in the morning where they are."

Standing on shaky legs, she motioned for him to follow her. "I understand. I'll set up a time so you can meet with the executive chef to taste some samples. In the meantime, I'll email you the menus and prices. I think majority of them will go with your budget."

Once they made it to the lobby, Harper was halfway disappointed he had to leave, but she had a million things to do before the club opened. One was to remember how to breathe again.

Unlocking the door, she glanced up at the commanding man in her personal space who stared at her seductively, causing her heart to do somersaults. She hated strangers so close but decided to make an exception this one time. After all, the man wasn't exactly a stranger, right? She'd spent the last hour in his presence trying her hardest to listen to what he said while attempting not to drool. She inhaled his cologne so she wouldn't forget it, and snapped a mental picture of his alluring face so she could describe him to her best friend as well as remember him once drifting off to sleep.

"It was very nice meeting you, Harper Bennett," he said in a deep, low voice.

Well there goes remembering how to inhale and exhale. The way her name rolled off his tongue sent an electric current to zoom through every cell in her body. Luckily, she lived within walking distance of the club because a cold shower may be her next task.

"You, too." Gulping, panic washed over her when she thought Hunter was going to lower his mouth to hers as his eyes brushed over it. She swore she could feel his succulent lips and long tongue that she'd noted earlier on her. His strong, smooth hands could definitely join the party, and she'd invite his muscular chest, too. In fact, every inch of him could come and the image sent another charged current to bolt through her.

"I'll see you tomorrow evening, Ms. Bennett."

Once he left and the doors were secured, Harper bent down and took off her six-inch heels which brought her down to five-foot-three. Carrying them, she trekked over to the elevator and pressed her pass code to the private third floor which housed the executive offices. Dashing to hers in a daze, she shut the door and plopped in her gold leather chair that her brothers had named the Diva's Throne.

Harper was in utter disbelief of her thought process. In the time it had taken her to leave the lobby and crash into the chair, she'd managed to daydream about undressing Hunter for a long, hot shower. But who was she kidding? He was a well-traveled man that probably had a woman in every city he'd journeyed to. Of course he flirted with every pretty lady that crossed his path and she was simply next on the list. With that assumption she breathed somewhat easier. Becoming involved with a man always on the go wasn't on her agenda. She preferred stability and the peace of mind to sleep at night knowing that whomever she dated wasn't far away in another city screwing someone else.

Besides, the man probably hasn't even given me a second thought and is not showing up tomorrow night. Yet the more she tried to convince herself of that, the more she knew it was a lie. Hunter would be there, and she'd count every second until she saw him again.

Chapter Two

Hunter thumbed through the papers on the desk as he sat in front of his laptop Skyping with Cannon and four other high-level members of Doctors Unlimited. However, he wasn't listening at one-hundred percent to what they discussed. The conversation pertained to more doctors fresh out of medical school and a training program, but he managed to tune them out since it wasn't his division. Instead, his thoughts were all mixed up on the vibrant smile, stunning figure, and smooth, toffee-coated legs of Harper Bennett. He was knocked off guard when Harper told him who she was. He was expecting a man because of the name. Plus, it was a last minute appointment his assistant had set up.

Normally, he'd researched who he was meeting with in advance, but he'd returned from a long flight the night before from Thailand and was operating on little sleep thanks to jetlag. However, settling his gaze on her gorgeous face for the first time woke him from tiredness and tossed him into a blissful abyss as an uncanny rapture had raged through him. He'd become so aware of her beauty and sexiness from the initial stare that he'd found it hard to recall why he was at Club Masquerade in the first place.

He was drawn to her almond-shaped, cat-like fiery eyes that had scanned over him briefly like an x-ray before settling upon his face. He'd noted the subtle rise of her delicate breasts under her silky pink blouse, and her fingers running through her bouncy array of back-length curls which symbolized she was fully aware of his immediate attraction to her. Her succulent, rose-painted lips had parted into a sultry smile, and when she spoke it soothed him like passionate sex and jazz on a rainy night. He'd noted the pearl necklace around her neck with the matching clasp bracelet that signified her refined elegance. However, he sensed another side of her that was anything but refined when he caught her dark brown eyes turning even darker as they quickly glanced under his belt.

Harper was petite and dainty in stature, but her over-confident and sassy personality made her appear taller and in charge. Of course her heels added height to what he figured a five-foot-four frame and enhanced her cute, little rump and curvy hips that settled provocatively in the straight skirt. He'd tried to stay focused on planning the fundraiser, but how could he when her captivating scent filled the atmosphere and every word that flowed from her kissable mouth poured out like warm honey journeying down his throat?

Hunter was rather surprised he'd asked her out. He didn't date, or at least not exclusively. That always created complicated situations over the years, and he'd broken a few hearts along the way. His career required him to drop everything without a second's notice and jet to the next city that needed him. He was in charge of overseeing that everything ran smooth with the organization. He was Cannon's right-hand man and trusted with making sure nothing was amiss. Hunter took his position very seriously. He had no connections as far as a wife and kids and never felt guilty about shooting off to the next country. Of course he missed his parents and his siblings, but he always made an effort to visit Memphis when he was in the States.

Hunter knew one day he would have to settle down in one location if he ever wanted a chance at having a family of his own. Cannon had made the suggestion several times over the past few years, but Hunter loved his freedom. He enjoyed his life of being hands on and helping others. He wasn't a doctor, but he was trained in basic first aid and he'd learned other medical procedures to help patients when the times arose in crisis or epidemic situations.

However, meeting Harper reminded him that he missed the sincere smile, the tantalizing, lingering scent, and the warm, silky skin of a woman. Like her, he never mixed business with pleasure, but asking her out seemed to be the natural thing to do. And while she didn't agree to a date, she did invite him back to the club the next evening. To him that was a positive step in the direction he wanted to travel. He'd never been a clubber, or at least not a club like Masquerade. He preferred the blues and jazz clubs that he frequented when he was home in Memphis or oversees if time permitted. Though if seeing her again meant listening to the latest hip hop and rap songs that he barely knew, then he would be there just to see her sexy strut and the swish of her hips that were on the same beat of a bass drum.

Reality came slowly back as Hunter frowned and then forced out a knowing smile along with a nod as if he knew what was happening on the computer in front of him. The other members of Doctors Unlimited were saying their good-byes and logging off the conference call, leaving Cannon with a peculiar grin and a questioning, raised eyebrow.

"Are you all right, man?" Cannon asked, sipping from a mug and setting it down on the desk in front of him. "You stared off into space for a moment."

This is why I hate FaceTime, Hunter thought. "Nah, man. Listening to you guys." And thinking about the beauty with the smile that could make the sun shine at night.

"So, is everything all set for the fundraiser event?"

"Yep, just left Masquerade and arranged all the details with the event planner." It was on the tip of his tongue to say *sexy* event planner, but he managed to hold it in.

"Isn't that a night club?" Cannon asked with a slight grimace.

"Don't worry, man. It's very swank and posh. It's an upscale establishment. Besides, it will be closed to the public. They do a lot of charity events when possible."

"Great. Yasmine and I are hoping to make it. I've been in contact with some of our big whale donors and they're onboard for the new clinic and the stateside headquarters in Atlanta." Cannon paused as a serious expression washed over his face. "You know the offer still stands for you to run the US headquarters, right?"

Normally, Hunter would say no but something pulled at his heart strings. He brushed it aside and changed the subject before he got ahead of himself with the silly notion of thinking that Harper Bennett was somehow factored into the equation called his life.

"How's Yaz and Mia?" he asked, referring to Cannon's wife and their six-year-old daughter.

"They're both well. I saw your parents at my parents' estate this afternoon. Your folks are excited and relieved that you're in the States for the time being."

"Yeah, my mother can rest easy at night knowing I'm not halfway across the world rescuing people from a tsunami." He'd spent the last week doing exactly that. "But I'm coming to Memphis next month to visit."

"I know the feeling because at the same time they're proud of you for wanting to help but terrified something could happen to you as well. Every time I leave I always promise my mom and Yaz that I'll return unscathed. Of course, I don't go as much as I used to with running

Arrington Family Specialists and dealing with other aspects of Doctors Unlimited, but I miss it sometimes. I honestly do. That's why I conceived the idea in medical school in the first place. My mission was to help as many people as possible."

"And look at it now. You've made a difference, big cuz."

"Thanks, man. I'm going to run and help put Mia to bed. It's my turn to read the bedtime story."

"All right. Talk to you soon."

Shutting the lid to his laptop, Hunter stood from the desk and plopped down on the couch in the sitting area of his hotel room at Pinnacle Boutique Hotel. The hotel was located in midtown Atlanta, a short cab ride away from Club Masquerade and away from Harper. Wrinkling his brow, he wondered how the hell that thought had jumped into his brain. However, Harper's face hadn't left his thoughts and as he grabbed the remote to turn to ESPN, the scent of the perfume that had lingered on his hand from their handshake whiffed to his nose. A naughty smile crossed his face as he grabbed his iPad seated on the cushion next to him, logged in online, and typed *Harper Bennett*. No, he wasn't a stalker. He would've done this before his appointment with her and been better prepared knowing he was meeting a Ms. Bennett not a Mr. Bennett. Even though now he had to admit that what he was doing could be considered borderline stalkerish.

Hunter came across a picture of the Bennett triplets at an event. Harper appeared even shorter standing in between her two brothers who appeared to be around his height at six-foot-two. She was breathtaking in a black, mini cocktail dress with her hair swept up in a tousled, messy but sexy style that enhanced her sharp cheekbones and her alluring eyes that he could definitely find himself becoming lost in and not wanting to be found. He stumbled upon another picture of her by herself from the same occasion that showcased her toned, muscular legs even better than the skirt she had on today.

A beep from his cell phone startled him, and he was highly surprised and elated that it was from Harper. He'd placed her cell number in his phone on the cab ride back to the hotel and he'd had to stop himself from dialing her. It was a short text stating she'd emailed him the menu and if he had any questions to call. As he read it, another message from her popped up that ended with a smiley face.

Looking forward to seeing you tomorrow night. :)

A sly grin emerged as he typed: **Ditto, beautiful one.**

*****

"What the hell did I text?" Harper asked herself out loud, pacing back in forth in her office. *It was supposed to be a business text. Hell, it was supposed to be a business meeting!*

The vibrating cell phone in her hand startled her, and she glanced down to see his response. *Beautiful one?* He'd called her that earlier and it had to be the sweetest term of endearment any man had ever called her—especially when he said it in such a sexy and seductive manner. Then she'd made the mistake of reading the text in his voice. Her heart vibrated faster than her phone and breathing correctly no longer seemed like the easiest thing to do. She'd never hyperventilated, but she had a strong notion that she was doing just that. What had she started? No, wait, what Hunter started by asking her out. Regardless, she wasn't supposed to continue it. She was supposed to nip it in the bud immediately.

She found herself beelining to the computer, typing in his name in the internet search engine, and tapping her foot on the white marbled floor of her French provincial decorated office. Nothing wrong with a little harmless research. Right?

A few articles popped up about the organization, including a recent one on the building of the clinic along with a headquarters office in Atlanta. Apparently, Hunter was overseeing the project for the next few months and stated in the interview that "I can't wait until it's complete so I can go to another locale and do the same".

And with that comment it reminded her that he was off-limits. A big no-no in order to protect her heart. She didn't want to start dating him, like him more than she should, then he left, and she never saw or heard from him again. Yet when she clicked on another link, Harper found several pictures of him that had her side eying her rule. His official picture on the Doctors Unlimited page caused her to bite her bottom lip as heat puddled in her center. The blue suit he wore fit his immaculate frame as if it was made exclusively for him. His smooth, delectable skin was indeed appetizing, and she craved to know how sweet the chocolate tasted.

Exhaling, she chastised herself for carrying on about a man that she couldn't date. She scrolled through some more photos and one pulled at her heart so strong that tears welled in her eyes. In the picture, Hunter carried a young boy he'd rescued who had lost his parents in a hurricane and unfortunately had to have his leg amputated because a heavy beam had fallen on it. The caption stated that Hunter stayed and comforted the child during the entire ordeal and then traveled with him the following week to his grandparents' home in another country to make sure he arrived there safely.

Wiping back another tear, she closed the laptop lid and prayed hard that she wouldn't fall for him. However, a compassionate, kindhearted man like Hunter impressed her because her brothers and her father were as well. She hated shallow, egotistical, arrogant men who weren't concerned about the world around them and only cared about their well-being and no one else.

Sighing, she knew she was in need of advice and only one person could offer it honestly. She glanced at the clock and scrolled through her cell phone to call her best friend since they were ten years old, London Alexander, who had just finished the six o'clock news in Charlotte, North Carolina.

"Hey, bestie!" London answered in a chipper tone. "Surprised you're calling at this time."

"Yeah. I need to go down to the main floor soon to meet with some of my staff but I have about twenty minutes …" She sighed as her voice trailed off.

"I hear it in your voice. What's wrong?"

"I met someone … well, not really. I mean possibly, but he doesn't live in Atlanta and you know I hate long-distance relationships. Not that I want a relationship with him, but there's something about him that intrigues me to the point that I haven't stopped smiling since I met him."

"You? Smiling at work? Don't let the employees see that," London teased.

"Now you remind me. I swear I don't know what's coming over me. I'm behaving like a lovesick teenager over the popular jock that finally noticed me."

"Uh huh. Soooooooo go out with him anyway for the fun of it while he's in town. No harm in that if you have chemistry."

"He asked me out, but I told him no because he's a client and I don't date clients. But then I kind of invited him to the club tomorrow night."

How the hell did she even think that inviting him to the club tomorrow night was a smart thing to do? Even when she had boyfriends she hated when they came because she was at work and sometimes her job meant being extra nice and smiling extra pretty at the ballers and celebrities that frequented. Her boyfriends took it as flirting when she would hug or wink at the handsome— and even the not so handsome—men. She didn't want them. And they didn't want her. It was all in fun. They respected her and more so her overprotective brothers to never mess with her. She was hands off. Plain and simple.

"Okay, you must really like him if you invited him to the club. Isn't that a no-no rule for you?"

"Yes, and you know how I am about sticking to my dating rules."

"Well, rules are made to be broken."

"And you should know," Harper teased, thinking about all the wild and crazy things they'd gotten into when they were younger.

"Ha, ha," London retorted in a tone laced with sarcasm. "Well, this guy must be drop dead gorgeous and fit all the criteria on your list."

"Every. Single. One. And guess what? He has a twin brother. We can double date."

"Oh my. Where does your possible new suitor live?"

"No set place. He's from Memphis, but he works for Doctors Unlimited and travels all over the world."

"I did a story on that organization a few years back. Hmm, now I understand your reservations. But again, have some fun. You used to be fun."

Taken aback, she scrunched her brow. "Excuse me? I'm still fun. You know our motto. Work hard. Play hard."

"Harp, you are at that club all the time. Even when you're off you're there."

"Not true." *Okay, that's a lie.*

"You're supposed to be at work at four. What time did you arrive there today?"

"Noon, but I had a gazillion tasks to do."

"And what time are you leaving tonight?"

"I don't know." She shrugged. "Three perhaps. There's a celebrity birthday and a few other private parties." Even though she had a trusted staff, Harper was a perfectionist and wanted to oversee everything. Carrying on her parents' legacy was very important to her and her brothers.

"And then right back at noon?"

"Maybe … if need be."

"Mmm-hmm. Exactly, and tomorrow is your off day. I'm not saying marry the brother. Just have a little fun."

"We'll see. So enough about me. What about you? Is everything okay?"

London remained silent except for a long sigh that erupted, and Harper knew her girl still worried about the crazy ex-boyfriend that used to stalk her.

"I'm hanging in there, but I need a change of scenery. I've decided to take Hot Atlanta News up on their job offer. I'm moving back to Atlanta at the end of next month."

"Oh, perfect! You can crash with me until you find a place. I miss you being in the ATL. It's not the same without you."

A familiar knock on Harper's door jerked her head toward it. "Hold on, L. Come in, Mase," she called out.

Her big brother by one minute stuck half his upper body inside with one of his favorite gourmet lollipops in his mouth which kept him calm when he was stressed. Harper figured he'd had a long day considering he was in the process of updating the security system for the club.

Mase slid the candy out to speak. "Harp, do you have a moment? I need to meet with you and Cam to go over a new security protocol before we open. Say in ten minutes by the second-floor bar?"

"I'll be there. I'm finishing up with London."

Harper swore she caught a tiny sparkle in her brother's eye at the mention of her best friend's name.

"Tell her I said what's up," he requested, before shutting the door closed.

"My brother says hello," she passed on, wearing a wide grin.

"Mmm-hmm … I heard."

Harper imagined her friend running a hand through her pixie-cut and then wrinkling her nose in frustration from messing it up considering she had to go back on the air tonight.

"So you know he's back for good. No more tours of duty." Even though Harper sensed that Mason wanted to but after having reconstructive surgery on his right hand, chin, and jaw during his last tour, he was discharged honorably. That had been a little over a year ago, and six months ago he decided it was time to finally work at the club he owned.

"You've told me several times in the last few months."

"Simply reminding you. Didn't you say Mase looked hot in his uniform? Of course, now his uniform consists of a black suit, but I'm sure you'll think he's still hot. But anyway, Mason is here ... so burrowing the bug in your ear. Again."

While Harper tried not to play matchmaker, she wanted her brother and her best friend happy and preferably happy together. They'd always had a brother-sister type bond even though at one point Harper sensed that it changed as they grew older. London grew up next door to the Bennetts and Mason, who rarely showed any emotion outside of his immediate family, always had a soft spot for her because her parents were killed when she was only ten and was raised by her grandparents.

"I'm ignoring you, Harp. Gotta run. I'll see you soon."

After hanging up, Harper retreated to the powder room in her office to reapply what little make-up she wore and fix a few loose curls. Taking a deep breath, she placed on her work-attitude cap and reminded herself that her thoughts could not for any reason float to Hunter Arrington. And just as she said the affirmation to herself in the mirror a wide, Cheshire Cat smile emerged.

Chapter Three

Harper's eyes scanned the club as she stood on the second floor peering down at the crowded dance floor. The DJ played a smash up of hits for Wind Down Wednesday and she found herself involuntarily rocking to the beat of a rap song mixed with an R&B one. However, her focus wasn't on the music or the scenery in front of her. Instead, her stare stayed glued on the entrance from the lobby to the main floor. Happy hour was almost over and still no sign of Hunter. She hadn't heard from him and had made a conscious effort not to contact him at all that day. Even while she worked on the arrangements for his event, she refused to call for his opinion for the fear of sounding like a rambling fool on the phone.

Out of the corner or her eye, she noticed one of the cocktail waitresses, Misti, approach. Even though she wore a purple and green masquerade mask, Harper could tell that Misti had a raised eyebrow.

"Hey, Ms. Bennett. Surprised to see you here on a Wednesday night unless there's an A plus celebrity in the building."

Harper was off on Wednesdays and Sundays, but she'd stopped by around five to work on a few projects. Though it was an excuse to be present during happy hour to see Hunter.

"Is there something you need?" Harper asked in a dismissive manner.

"No. I'm surprised to see you," Misti replied, skirting away in haste to a table that had signaled her.

Placing her focus back on the scene below, Harper spotted the person she'd searched for the past hour gazing at her with a mischievous yet honest grin. She suddenly became very aware of her appearance as he raked his eyes over her body in one swoop. She'd taken extra care that afternoon in selecting her attire. A red, lacy dress that stopped at her knees, was accentuated with a classy gold bracelet and matching necklace. Big bouncy curls surrounded her face and cascaded below her shoulders, and a pair of red pumps completed her look. She didn't want to appear overly sexy, but she wanted to be beautiful to him considering she couldn't erase his comment of "beautiful one" out of her head.

Holding onto the rail in front of her for support, Harper watched as he strode over to the escalator. Her eyes roamed over his khaki dress slacks, and the way his butt sat nice and firm in them caused her to let out a soft moan. His blue dress shirt was unbuttoned at the top and showcased a peek of his chest, which looked more appetizing than any Hershey bar she'd ever eaten. She was somewhat disappointed he wore a black newsboy hat, but it was just as well because if she'd seen his bald head, the urge to reach out and travel a hand over it may have come into play. The thought sent a warm sensation to skate through her body and her heart to overbeat erratically.

Harper reminded herself over and over that she had to keep it professional with him. Unfortunately, her tossing and turning last night and the two cold showers after her morning jog only heightened the fact that she wanted to know more about him. She hadn't been this interested in a man in a long while ... if at all, and that scared her. Usually she was able to turn off any attraction when she knew it wouldn't work out.

Yes, Hunter was handsome, intelligent, and seemed like a very nice, down-to-earth man, but she feared that she'd fall for him more than she should. And then what? Emails, phone calls, and the occasional visit when he wasn't shooting off to another part of the world to offer his services to help save it? However, the genuine smile he bestowed to her when he jumped onto the escalator reminded her why she'd invited him in the first place. She had an inkling the smile she returned matched his.

Hunter didn't stand on one step. Instead his long legs skipped every other one. As soon as he stepped off, he dashed straight to her.

"Hello, Ms. Bennett," he greeted in a loud tone over the music. "You look amazing."

"Thank you, and so do you." Checking her watch, she glanced at the line at the upstairs bar. "You're just in time for a drink. Happy hour ends in ten minutes."

"I'm good," he replied, closing the small gap between them, and gave her a warm hug. "I didn't come for the drinks, beautiful one."

And there it was. That dang, charming term of endearment that would surely have her forget all the affirmations she'd made to herself and have a little fun as London had suggested. As she reluctantly pulled away from his secure embrace, she had to steady herself. Hunter's body was hard. Rigid. Sexy. Being encased by him for that short period of time awakened a feeling of pleasure and passion to explode through her. She fit snug and perfect in his muscular arms. His scent, which was now imbedded on her skin, was downright provoking.

Doesn't he realize I'm trying to resist him?

Backing a step away, Harper motioned for him to follow her to a nearby seating area that had been roped off. It contained oversized, comfy, white leather sofas and chairs that were flanked with purple, square tables. It was situated out of the way of the speakers and now she wouldn't have to scream at the man. Taking a seat in one of the chairs, she crossed her legs as he sat on the couch adjacent to her.

"So, as you can see the atmosphere is quite low-key on a Wednesday night, at least for now. There's an after-party for a concert later on so the place will be packed. But I figured happy hour was more your speed. You don't seem to be the club type, but a lot of professional women attend during this time."

"I'm not here to pick up women and drink."

A heat wave rushed across her skin at his words. She knew why he was there, but she had to have willpower and stay focused. Instead she nodded and darted her eyes away from him and straight into a security camera mounted on a column a few feet away. She hoped like hell that Mase wasn't in the security room watching her. The triplets knew each other's facial expressions and mannerisms better than anybody else. While she could hide what she was thinking from Hunter, there was no way she could hide it from her brothers.

Blinking her eyes and turning away from the camera, she put her professional cap on and prayed that it wouldn't blow off during their conversation. "There's different lighting effects depending upon the music, the night, the event, etc. I'm thinking for your event perhaps soft white and pale pink lights. I had the DJ try them out before we opened and it gave the club a really elegant feel for your fundraiser gala. I was also able to book the jazz band I was telling you about, but I think we should still use the DJ during the band's breaks. What do you think?"

"Whatever you suggest," he replied with a shrug.

"Also, since tulips are in season I can have my girl that creates amazing flower arrangements make elegant, classy centerpieces perhaps intertwined with peonies and some other pretty blooms. Maybe orchids."

"Are all those your favorite flowers?" he questioned.

"Um … peonies are my favorite. Preferably the pink and white ones."

"Good to know. And yes, that's fine for the centerpieces."

"Perfect. Also, I spoke to Josh, the bartender who will be working your event, and he's going to create a special peach cocktail for the evening. The man is a crazy mixologist. Probably why our drinks are voted best in Atlanta every year."

Chuckling, Hunter leaned in toward her and grabbed her hand. "I didn't come here to discuss business. I trust your judgment for the fundraiser, otherwise I would've gone elsewhere. I came to see you."

"Hunter, I need to be honest. I would love to hang out with you while you're in town, but I don't see the point of wasting your time, or mine, for something that isn't going to go anywhere. I'm too old for flings, one-night stands and such. You're a very-welled travelled man who probably has women in every country."

"Glad you think so highly of me … I think," he said in a sarcastic yet joking manner. "But I'm not an international player … well, not on purpose. I've had a few girlfriends here and there, but it's kind of hard with all the travelling I do to have a meaningful relationship."

"That's exactly why I can't go out with you."

"Listen." Rising, he walked over and knelt in front of her as the music became louder and the lights darkened to a deep purple. "Ever since I turned thirty-five, I've started thinking more and more about my future. Eventually, I want a wife and children in a stable environment. Trust me, I understand where you're coming from. I'm too old for flings and one-night stands as well. The thought of those with you never crossed my mind. There's something about you that I find endearing and I want to know why regardless of only being in Atlanta for the next few months. I need to know why I lost sleep last night. I need to know why I daydreamed about you all damn day. I need to know why you have me contemplating things I've never given a second thought to."

Suppressing the smile that wanted to emerge at his testimony, she withdrew her hand from his before she did the unthinkable. He was close enough to lay an erotic kiss on his delectable lips, and she knew he wouldn't mind at all. And she wouldn't regret it either. "Wow. That's pretty deep." *Considering I had those exact same thoughts.* "I think I need a drink," she chuckled nervously, rubbing her hand back and forth on her neck to cease the sweat that was forming before she became a puddle of water on the leather chair. "Maybe two."

"Well, that won't be hard to do here." He rose from his knee. "I can go grab one for you. What do you want?"

"Oh, no. I don't drink in front of the employees. Tell the bartender to make my usual mocktail." She nodded toward the bar. "And order whatever you want. It's on the house."

A sexy grin crossed his lips as he bent down and whispered in her ear, "What I want the bartender can't make unless you can squeeze your fine, sexy ass in one of those martini glasses."

Heat rushed to her face and the smile she'd compressed finally emerged. "Go grab the drinks, Hunter."

Once he left, she finally exhaled. The man caused emotions to swirl around and attack whatever common sense she had left. Which wasn't much at the moment as she contemplated whether or not to have fun with him while he was in town. It had been a long while since she'd met a nice guy like him. Who knows? They could be great friends … and yet the word "friend" wasn't what she wanted.

"Hey, pretty lady."

Frowning at the interruption of her deep, amorous thoughts, Harper peered up into the bloodshot eyes of a man towering over her. He was way too close and unfamiliar to her. She knew most of the regulars from happy hour as his orange wristband signified that he'd attended it. However, sometimes when conferences were in downtown, the club had an influx during Wind Down Wednesday as hotels in the area had Club Masquerade ads in their information booklets.

Standing, she backed out of his personal space, clasped her hands in front of her, and smiled politely. "Hello. Are you having a nice time this evening at Club Masquerade?" she asked in a professional tone which usually made men who approached her at the club back down and realize she more than work there.

"Yes, and I was hoping to have even a better time later on. Can I buy you a drink?"

"No, thank you. My boyfriend is handling that now." As soon as she said it, an uncanny feeling washed over her. *Boyfriend?* While that was her usual lie to ward men off, she almost believed it as she glanced at Hunter who was third in line at the bar.

"Mmm-hmm," he said as a snarl appeared. "I know you're lying. You were sitting here for at least five minutes by yourself." He stepped into her comfort zone. "I spotted you when I rode up the escalator."

Clearing her throat, Harper stepped away from him as his unappealing, cheap cologne and a whiff of alcohol filled her nostrils. "I'm not lying, and if I were you, I'd walk away right now and leave the premises." She silently chastised herself for leaving her earpiece in her office to contact security, but technically she was off tonight.

Grabbing her hand, he pulled her roughly toward him as she yanked away.

"You really shouldn't have done that," she stated in a calm yet stern manner.

"Why? Is your so-called boyfriend a black belt or something?"

"As a matter of fact, I am," a deep, firm voice stated.

A Passionate Night

A pleased smile crossed Harper's face as she turned to see Hunter standing behind her wearing a confident yet serious expression aimed at the bastard who'd bothered her.

Hunter moved her behind him and stepped in the unruly man's space. "Now, I really hate to cause a commotion in front of a lady; therefore, it's in your best interests to leave. She's been very nice to you. But me ..." Hunter paused, clenching his jaw. "I'm not so nice. And considering you had the fucking *audacity* to put your hands on *my* woman, I can't make any promises not to lay hands on you and not in a prayerful way either."

"Man, please," the bastard said, taking a swing at Hunter, who grabbed the man's fist, bent back his arm as a crunch sounded, and then placed him in a chokehold.

"Let me go, you punk," he said, trying to break loose but Hunter held him firm.

Impressed with Hunter's protection of her, Harper motioned for him to follow her to a private exit that was behind a drape not far from the sitting area. He followed while the man continued to struggle and yell out obscenities.

She shook her head with a smirk and addressed the unwanted guest. "Now see, you could've done this the easy way but you chose not to." Placing her thumb on the computerized scan pad, she opened the door and was startled but not surprised to see Mason and Cameron standing there as if they were ready to kill. They stepped back as Hunter pushed the man into the hallway that led to the second floor stairwell and the security monitoring center.

"That's right. You better let me go," the man huffed as he leaned against the wall, rubbing his neck. "Are y'all the managers? This asshole needs to be arrested for attacking me over this lame hoe."

Immediately the other three men rushed to him but Hunter yanked him by the collar first and raised him up off the floor as the brothers stood on either side.

"What the hell did you call my sister?" Cameron yelled out.

Gritting his teeth, Mason put his head closer to the scumbag's. "That's a death wish, and I don't have a problem making it come true."

"Guys, calm down," Harper pleaded. "I'm fine. Just throw him out of our club."

Two burly security guards approached the scene and Hunter let go of the man's collar, dropping him to the floor.

"Get this fool out of here," Cameron shouted as the guards ushered the unwanted guest toward the stairwell. "Are you all right, sis? We saw that jackass grab you on the monitors."

"I'm fine. Mase, check the monitors and see which bartender from downstairs didn't cut him off. That guy was wasted."

Mason nodded. "I will, but first, are you okay?"

"Yes, Hunter had it under control."

At the mention of his name, the brothers turned to Hunter as if really seeing him for the first time.

"Cam, Mase, this is Hunter Arrington. Remember I told you that Doctors Unlimited is having their fundraiser gala here."

Mason lifted his head in a "what's up" gesture as Cameron reached out and shook Hunter's hand. "Yes, of course." He glanced at Mason. "My brother and I appreciate you looking out for our sister."

Hunter shook Cameron's hand and turned as Mason reached out his hand as well. "No problem. Trust me, I have two baby sisters and I'd want someone to do the same for them."

"Well, we appreciate it. And to show my thanks, how about the next time you come you bring your lady, and I'll have a VIP area set up for you with food and bottle service all night on the house."

Shaking his head, Hunter waved his hands in front of him. "Not necessary." He glanced over at Harper with a sincere smile. "I'd do it again." He said it to Cameron but stared right at Harper.

Sensing her brothers' antennas rising, she scurried to Hunter's side and lightly pulled him by the elbow back to the door. "And I appreciated it. Gentlemen, I'll let you get back to business, and we're going to finish our meeting," she explained, noticing curious eyebrows and wrinkled foreheads from her brothers. "I'm leaving soon since technically I'm off today. So, I'll see you fellas tomorrow evening." With that she quickly opened the door and passed through with Hunter on her heel.

Plopping back on the couch, she glanced over her shoulder to see if her brothers had followed, but they hadn't and she breathed easy. While they didn't mind that she dated, they always interrogated the men she introduced them to—especially after she caught her ex cheating.

"Take it your brothers are overly overprotective?"

"I don't mind, but considering we aren't dating or anything, I didn't want them to initiate their usual question session. Well, Cam asks the questions like a detective while Mase paces around as if he's ready to kill with his bare hands. Of course, it has weeded out duds, but …"

"I'm no dud. I can handle myself."

"So I witnessed, and I truly appreciate it. Men rarely bother me at the club, but he wasn't a regular. So are you really a black belt?"

"Yep, Taekwondo. I started training in middle school. My parents thought I was somewhat of a wild card unlike Chase, my twin, who's very astute. My friends had started to hang with the wrong crowd and my parents feared I would as well. They figured I needed some type of disciplined activity so I took Taekwondo and played basketball."

"Cool. You'll have to show me some moves. I played softball and ran track in high school. Definitely kept me focused."

His eyes perused her calves and the bit of thigh that peeked from her dress. Harper swore she could feel the caress from his eyes glide on her skin in a seductive manner. She crossed her legs but that did nothing to simmer down the heat boiling in her center.

"Yes, I see you have runner legs. Do you still run?"

"I jog or do cardio on most days, or sometimes yoga or kickboxing. It all relieves tension."

A wicked smile crossed his face, and Harper could only imagine what fantasy had played in his brain. "How about that drink?" she reminded, changing the subject as she stood and he followed suit. *Another check. He stands when I stand.*

"I'll take care of it. You just relax."

"I need a real drink after that little fiasco. I know of this cool place within walking distance and they have really great drinks and delicious food. Besides, you need to explore some of Atlanta while you're here."

He raised a hopeful smile. "So you're going to be my private tour guide after all?"

Her answer was a flirty wink.

Chapter Four

Hunter opened the door of Café Intermezzo to let Harper cross the threshold, or in her case strut provocatively past him in six inch heels. She mouthed a sexy thank you as she entered and continued to the host stand where she gave the hostess a hug and asked for her usual area to sit. Even though he was a gentleman, he had to admit admiring her sultry body wrapped seductively in a lace red dress and her scent tickling his nose was enough to make him forget. His gaze wandered over her rounded hips and plump butt as they continued onto their table. He didn't notice any of the ambience or the patrons of the crowded restaurant. Nope, just the woman in front of him who'd finally decided to be his "tour guide".

Hunter had enjoyed every moment of watching her walk the few blocks to the restaurant as she'd pointed out places along the way—places he couldn't remember because he wasn't listening. He was too busy admiring her ass swishing in front of him, and imagining all the ways her legs could be intertwined with his.

Pulling out her chair, he lingered his eyes on her adorable face. She wore little make-up which was fine with him. She was a natural beauty with warm, toffee-colored skin that he had an urge to glide his tongue over and taste the sweetness radiating from her. A slight strain pressed against his pants at the erotic thought. Remembering he was wearing spring khakis, he pushed in her chair and immediately plopped into his seat across from her.

A waitress stopped by to greet them with two glasses of water and promised to return in a few moments with the cocktails they'd ordered.

"So, what do you recommend from the menu?" he asked, picking up his in the hopes of pulling his mind out of the gutter.

Harper raised her eyes up from her perusal of the menu and settled them on him. For the first time he noticed the place was dimly lit and the candle on the table illuminated her face beautifully. No, he didn't think his mind was rising from the gutter any time soon. More like drowning in it, like he was at that moment as her smoldering stare rested on him inquisitively.

"Well, what are you in the mood for?" she asked.

Chuckling, he closed the menu and leaned in toward her. Grabbing one of her hands, he set it on the table under his. He licked his tongue over his bottom lip and whispered, "Toffee. Rich toffee."

Her lips slid into an amused smirk, and she glanced at the extensive dessert display case that contained cheesecakes, pastries, and other sweet treats. He decided to play along and peek there as well for a quick second. The only sweet thing he wanted sat across from him wearing a sensual expression on her face. Goodness, he hoped he'd have a chance to see more of it and he hoped to be the reason.

Closing her eyes halfway, she released a moan. "Mmm, they do have a toffee cheesecake. It's so freakin' delish." Biting her bottom lip, Harper squeezed his hand. "It's rich. Creamy. Smooth. Mmm … I think you'd enjoy indulging in it."

Travelling his fingers up her bare forearm and back down to her hand, Hunter loved watching her eyelashes flutter at the gesture. She let out a long, seductive sigh and shifted in her seat. Aroused by the feel of her warm skin under his, sent his pulse to race like a car speeding in the Indy 500.

"Hmm … I may have to indulge in it, as you suggested. Sounds absolutely delicious, beautiful one."

"It is." Removing her hand and leaning back into her chair, she reopened her menu and continued reading it. "You should order it."

Wrapping his legs around hers under the table, an arrogant grin reached his face when she sucked in her breath. "I wasn't talking about the dessert."

"Oh, I know," she answered matter-of-factly. "Neither was I."

"So, you want to leave now?" he asked seriously, scooting his chair back.

"No. The cheesecake will have to satisfy you. Besides, I'm hungry."

"I'm hungry, too, but it damn sure ain't for anything on this menu."

"Down, boy. I was teasing you."

He chuckled and took a sip of his water even though he wished the waitress would hurry the hell up and return with his martini. "So you were flirting with me?"

"Perhaps," she answered with a wink. "I mean after all you started it with craving all this *toffee* seated across from you."

"I have from the moment we met."

"Most men do but that doesn't mean you're getting me. Besides, you're only here for a few months."

"But you decided to go out with me anyway."

"This isn't a date, remember? I wanted to thank you for handling that scumbag."

"No, you wanted to see where this can go."

"It's not going anywhere, sweetheart. You don't live here, and I don't do long distance relationships ..."

The word *anymore* popped into his head. Hunter nodded in awareness as he now realized Harper's gripe and it had nothing to do with him. "Ahhh, let me guess. Some dumbass brother ruined it for everyone else. He cheated and you found out."

"Yep, the hard way. Tried surprising him for his birthday after he said he couldn't come to Atlanta because of a last minute business meeting that he couldn't cancel. I decided to fly to New York and got a surprise of my own as I opened his brownstone door with the key he gave me. But something in my gut had warned me he was dating someone else. I needed to see for myself. The sad thing is she wasn't even an upgrade. If you're gonna cheat fine, but at least find someone more drop dead gorgeous and finer than me."

"Well, he didn't know what a gem he had. But, Harper, I'm not him. I've never cheated on any of my girlfriends. I'm not that kind of man."

"Never said you were. I'm not bitter or heartbroken. It hasn't turned me off from dating or made me think that all men are assholes who can't be trusted. That incident simply informed me of what I don't want. I don't see the point of wasting my time."

"But here you are."

"Don't flatter yourself."

"Hmm ... didn't I hear you tell your brothers you were off today? Yet there you were at the club." A cocky smirk inched up his jaw and he leaned toward her. "You wanted to see me, huh?"

She shrugged nonchalantly. "It's not uncommon for me to stop by on my off days if I need to. I had a few calls to make for your event."

"And you couldn't make a few phone calls in the comfort of your own home?"

Swishing her lips to the side, Harper cut her eyes at him. "I needed to check on some other things as well."

"In a sexy red dress and heels? Not that I mind. A little overdressed, don't you think? Considering it's your off day."

"Whatever. Believe what you want. I always dress up when I'm at the club. Otherwise, I prefer to be casual and comfy in jeans and flats."

"I bet you look fine in jeans, too."

"Sure do," she answered with a confident smile.

The waitress returned with their cocktails and jotted down their orders. He ordered the pecan-crusted chicken while Harper ordered the slow-cooked beef.

"You seem to know everyone in here," he commented after the waitress left but not without giving Harper a warm hug.

"Mostly. This is one of my favorite places to unwind. I love the food and the atmosphere."

"So you have all your dates bring you here?" he teased. "No wonder the entire staff knows you."

"Ha! You're not a date, and no. I usually come alone or pick up a sandwich to go."

"I love how you keep reminding me that this isn't a date. However, the evening is young and who knows what may happen between now and tomorrow morning."

"You don't give up."

"Do you want me to?"

Her eyes darkened and her legs tightened around his. "No," she whispered.

*****

Harper replayed their conversation from the evening over and over in her head as they strolled along Peachtree Street while she pointed out different places of interests such as the Fox Theatre. Her arm linked with Hunter's was comforting and secure as he walked next to the sidewalk. She loved the fact that he was a gentleman, even though after their heated flirting she had to admit she wouldn't mind knowing the un-gentleman side of him as well. When he'd held her hand down on the table, the thought of being intertwined with him and naked in her bed while he held both of her hands firmly on the mattress had filled her head.

The margarita she'd ordered couldn't arrive fast enough to calm down her amorous visions. She hadn't even kissed the man yet, but her thoughts had soared far beyond that. Some of them weren't even sexual. It was just being with him in a carefree way. For example, now as she wore the flip flops that she kept in her purse while he carried her heels because her feet had begun to hurt from walking on the concrete. Normally, she'd suck it up on a date, especially a first one, but she felt comfortable enough with him to be herself. It was a wonderful feeling, and even though she'd stated she didn't want to waste her time with him, she wasn't. No matter what happened, Harper was thankful that she'd met a man like him.

They stopped in the front of the Pinnacle Boutique Hotel, and she stared up at him as a wide smile filled his ruggedly handsome face.

"You know this is where I'm staying while I'm in town, right?"

"You'll have to eat that cheesecake by yourself." Pausing, Harper nodded her head toward the to-go bag in his other hand. "I'm not coming up."

"I wasn't asking you to."

"Well, thank you for being respectful."

"I didn't say I didn't want to. I'm just not going to."

"That's good to know. But can you walk me to my place? I walked to the club since it was a nice, spring evening. My home is a few blocks from here and no, you're not coming up."

"I know how to wait for something precious, beautiful one."

"That's sweet, but who said you needed to wait for something you're never gonna have?"

"It's this little thing called hope."

"Ha, well keep hoping," she teased.

Once they arrived in the contemporary-styled decorated lobby of The Lofts on Peachtree, Harper was somewhat disappointed that she wasn't inviting him up. She wasn't ready for the evening to end. The angel wearing white on her left shoulder kept screaming 'no, girl, don't let him up' but the angel wearing black on her right shoulder whispered 'what's the harm, girlfriend?'

"Can you walk me to my door? After all, you are a gentleman, right?" *He doesn't have to come in. He doesn't have to come in,* she chanted over and over in her head.

"So you're asking me up, huh?" he asked.

They walked toward the private elevator to her floor that had the only penthouse apartment. She preferred her privacy so she'd bought all three lofts and converted them to one three thousand square feet space. Mason—being concerned for her safety—had installed cameras and a high-tech security system a few years back.

She submitted her key card and the doors opened. Stepping inside with Hunter, her mind floated back to her image of lying underneath him once more. Being in close proximity to him caused her heart to beat erratically and a heat wave to wash over her body. Goodness, she wanted this man. Everything about him screamed the sex would be amazing. Passionate. Mind blowing. But she didn't want a sexual relationship. He would be the kind of man she'd fall for and then he'd leave on his next mission. She'd never been heartbroken before, but for some reason her chest tightened at the notion, which was why she had to protect herself. He could hope all he wanted to but nothing could happen between them.

"So no elevator music?" he teased.

"No, and thank goodness. After listening to loud club music all night, it's a peaceful ride up twelve floors to my home."

The doors opened to the hallway that was flanked with abstract paintings from local artists she supported. She locked the elevator and proceeded to pause in front of the double stainless steel doors of her home. Hunter's chest meshed against her back and her stomach contracted with anticipation. While he wore a shirt and probably a T-shirt underneath, she could only feel the pure hardness of his body. The heat from him radiated through her and his quietness along with the subtle way he cleared his throat spoke volumes. Harper's breathing and self-discipline quickly unraveled, and while she tried to conjure up more willpower, it was no use when Hunter whispered her name in an adoring, sensual way.

Rotating around to face him, she met his hot gaze as she rested her back against the door. She dropped her purse to the hardwood floor, and he followed suit with her shoes and the to-go bag. Running a finger down her cheek, he settled it on her mouth that parted and she kissed it softly. A slow, seductive smile drew across his face, and she knew there was no turning back. Her heart screamed yes, but her head screamed no and she always followed the latter. However, not this time.

Yanking her by the waist to him, Hunter smashed his lips against hers as she welcomed the kiss she'd craved from the moment she'd laid eyes on his enticing, tempting mouth. His tongue met hers in a seductive salsa over and over, causing moans she didn't recognize as her own to escape from her throat. They were mixed with his intense groans, and she loved the symphony they composed. She tossed his hat off and ran her hands up to his smooth, bald head and back down to his face as the intensity of their passion amplified with each passing second. The surreal feelings rushing through her body unraveled all the common sense she'd had at the beginning of the evening. Now she was where she wanted and needed to be: wrapped in his warm embrace.

"You taste way better than that damn cheesecake," he groaned on her lips before delving back into her mouth once more.

"I told you that you'd enjoy it."

"And you were right. You're driving me crazy, woman."

His hands journeyed firmly down her side and slipped around to her butt with a hard squeeze. She clenched his shoulders at the same time for the fear of falling over as his manly physique pressed hard against her. She couldn't fathom being anymore close to him than she already was. They were super glued together and nothing could be wedged between them.

Kissing Hunter was even more passionate than she'd imagined. He awakened emotions and desires in her that had been suppressed thanks to the Great Wall of China she'd placed around her heart. She'd dated and had a couple short relationships since her ex in New York, but she would never let them near her heart. Now Harper's emotions blossomed with an overzealous fervor that wouldn't shut off. It caused her to fall into an abyss of an unknown universe that waited for her, and she yearned to experience it only with Hunter.

The passion soaring through her veins made her high and alive. She loved the way he'd turn up their tempo with wild, untamed kisses that she matched with every stroke. Then they'd simmer down to sweet, savory brushes across her lips that made her ache for more fervent kisses. Hunter was in control of their tryst, and for once she didn't mind offering the reins to someone else. Harper loved being in control of every aspect of her life but not at this moment. His commanding touch wreaked havoc on her system, and she would need a valium to calm down her soaring high.

Her center filled with heat at the very notion of him being there indulging in her essence just as she'd suggested at dinner. She couldn't believe she'd been that forward with him, especially on the first date that wasn't a date. Or least that's what she wanted to convince herself of. Nevertheless, after she witnessed Hunter handling the scumbag in the club, it turned her on so fierce she needed to be alone with him. Crazy, sexual thoughts of him handling her body with the hands that had protected her drove her insane. Now she experienced it and loved his tender as well as rough-in-a-wonderful way caress on her.

His lips left hers and trailed gentle, succulent bites down her neck. A disappointed cry shrieked from her because she didn't want him to leave her mouth. Although, at the same time she longed to know what else he could do with his lethal tongue.

Hunter chuckled quietly at her response. Raising his head back to Harper, he kissed her forehead and landed a soft smooch on her lips. "I'm not done ravaging you," he informed her with clenched teeth as his eyes darkened from light brown to a deep chocolate. "I can't get enough of your erotic moans in my ear, beautiful one."

"Mmm … then don't stop anytime soon so you can continue to hear them, handsome one."

She collided her lips against his and this time she controlled the intensity of their ardent adventure. He didn't seem to mind as she pulled his tongue farther into her mouth with deep, winding circles. His manhood pulsed against her and a tremble charged through every inch of her body. Yanking the hem of her dress up to her thighs, he intertwined his finger with the band of her lacy thong. Her breath wedged in her throat as she thought for sure he would pull her panties down and then there could be no way she would reject anything he requested. However, he didn't as his hands roamed back up her side and massaged her breasts. In a way she was grateful that he possessed more willpower than her. She wasn't supposed to ask him up but she had. Heck, she wasn't even supposed to go to dinner with him but she did, and there were no regrets from her. Especially considering the man knew how to kiss her as if she belonged only to him.

"Maybe we should take this inside," he muttered against her lips. "I wouldn't want the neighbors calling the police.

"We can, but I don't have any neighbors. I own the entire floor."

Hunter glanced around the hallway. "There's cameras and another door," he stated, nodding his head in its direction.

"I'm the only one who has access to the hallway cameras but not the elevator one. The door leads to my private rooftop terrace. You can see downtown from up there."

He raised a curious eyebrow. "But can *we* be seen?" he asked, biting his bottom lip.

Harper snickered at his question and at the ideas that were probably running rampant in his dirty mind. Okay, and in hers as well. "*We* aren't going up there tonight, but we can go inside."

"Will the kissing continue inside?" he asked, gliding his tongue around her ear and to the side of her neck.

A soft purr emerged from her, and Harper had to restrain herself from yelling out what she really wanted to say to him. However, if she was going to hang out with him even after blatantly informing him and herself that she didn't mix business with pleasure, she had to exercise some restraints.

"No. I think we should leave that out here."

Turning her around, he lifted up her hair which elicited a pleased moan to escape her. He wrapped his other hand around her waist and meshed her against him. "Then we'll stay for a moment longer." Hunter landed his lips on the back of her neck in an intoxicating kiss. "Is that all right with you?" he asked, gliding his hand up to her breasts.

"Um … a few … more minutes … um … mmm … won't hurt," she managed to stutter out as he continued the enticing assault on her neck. He glided his tongue around to her collarbone, her shoulders, and then captured her mouth in a slow, deep kiss. Her emotions were spiraling out of control with pure pleasure, and she steadied herself against him while trying to ignore his erection on her backside. This was all so wrong and so unlike her, but the carefree feeling of their intense ecstasy drowned out all of her common sense as she found herself freefalling into a breathtaking oblivion.

Turning around to face him, she smiled when Hunter pushed her hair behind her ears. She knew it had to be a wild bird's nest thanks to him playing in it, but she didn't care. He stared down at her as he swayed with her back and forth to a soft melody that only they could hear.

"You are an amazing woman, and I'm not going to lie, I want you right now. But I promised to be a gentleman even though I guess I did sort of break that, huh?"

"It's fine. I enjoyed myself immensely."

"Me too."

"You can still come in, though," she suggested. "You can eat your cheesecake."

He pressed his lips together and rested his forehead on hers. "Please tell me you're referring to the dessert in the bag."

She lightly punched him on the upper arm. "There goes your perverted thinking again. Not that I mind. And yes, I was referring to the dessert."

"Okay. I'll be good," he promised, raising his right hand. "Scout's honor."

Sliding her hands off of him, she stooped down for her purse and rustled around until she found her keys. Opening the door, she flicked on the light switch which turned on three small chandeliers in the foyer hallway.

"You can leave mine and your shoes by the door."

She set her purse on the wood chair by the credenza and strolled into the living area. It was one large room with a stainless steel, industrial galley kitchen along one long wall which faced the dining and the living area. Antique-white sofas and chairs flanked with light gray, oversized toss pillows, glass coffee tables to match the six-seater glass dining table, and huge white candles sat in tall hurricanes. At times she replaced them with fresh flowers such as roses or peonies.

Her heartbeat sped up as she heard him shut the doors and his shoes hit the walnut wood floors. Inviting him inside wasn't on tonight's agenda, but she wasn't ready for the evening to end either. Taking a deep breath, she turned around and found him in the kitchen standing behind the stainless steel island opening the bag with the two slices of cheesecake.

He smiled as his eyes perused the living area and landed on the closed opaque sliding doors as if he knew what was on the other side.

"Is there a television in there?" he asked, setting the to-go box on the counter.

There was a flat screen on her bedroom wall, but she wasn't going to divulge that tidbit of information.

She headed toward the cabinets in the kitchen and pulled out two saucers. "I have a media room down the hall," she answered, taking two forks out of the drawer. She placed everything on the island. "Third door on the right. I'll meet you there in a moment. Going to change into something more comfortable. And before your brain drowns in the gutter, by comfortable I mean sweats not sexy lingerie."

"I'm sure you're adorable and sexy in anything you wear."

"Oh, so I can put on my avocado face mask as well?" she teased, pivoting on her heel and walking toward the master bedroom suite.

"If that's the only thing you're going to wear?"

He asked in a joking manner, but she had an inkling he was halfway serious. Shaking her head at him, she slid one of the doors back and slipped in before shutting it quickly.

Unzipping her dress, she let it fall to the floor and made her way over to her expansive bathroom and closet that at one point had been one of the loft apartments. However, she had a ton of clothes, purses, and shoes and each needed their own separate space in her neatly organized and color-coordinated shelves. A huge island with ten drawers on each side contained her comfy casuals as well as her lingerie. Laughing off her ridiculous thoughts of teasing him with a sexy nightgown, she pulled out black yoga pants along with a Howard University sweat shirt and slipped them on. Grabbing a scrunchie from one of the drawers, she pulled her hair into a messy ponytail at the top of her hair. She didn't even bother to glance in the mirror. Instead, she said a little prayer on the way to the media room that she could make it through the rest of the evening without wanting to continue … or rather finish what they'd started, followed by cooking him breakfast in the morning.

Chapter Five

When Harper stepped into the media room, Hunter's eyes were instantly drawn to her fiery ones and her luscious lips that were plump at the moment from their tryst earlier. Even in sweats, no make-up, and a messy updo, she still possessed a sexiness to her that exuded confidence and charm that never shut off. That impressed him, as well as how passionate she was during their first kiss. He'd had quite a few first kisses but none that shook him to his core and stayed on his mind and lips.

Hunter knew he shouldn't have come up to her loft, and had debated his decision in the elevator ride. His plan was to make sure she got in safely, kiss her cheek or forehead, and then skedaddle back to his hotel for a long, cold shower. However, the sultry way she'd rested her eyes on him along with the subtle rise and fall of her chest, signified she wanted him at that very moment. Of course he had to oblige and make her happy. Right? Harper Bennett wasn't the kind of woman to be refused, and he wanted nothing more than to please her.

Her lips on his had surged so much passion and desire to coast freely through him that he couldn't explain his own emotions. What he'd begun to feel for her was uncanny and refreshing. They'd just met, but kissing her for the first time wasn't awkward or odd as it had been with other women. No, kissing Harper seemed natural and familiar. Peaceful in a way. They were in sync from the second his lips touched hers and for a moment time had stood still. If he didn't know any better, he thought for sure her lips were created exclusively to kiss him and only him.

While Hunter completely understood her disdain for long distance relationships, at the same time he knew he wouldn't be able to stay away now that he'd kissed his *beautiful one*. He didn't even know where in his brain he'd snatched that term of endearment. Most of the time he called women he was interested in or dating baby or babe. Beautiful one fit Harper perfectly considering she was the most beautiful woman he'd ever laid eyes on.

He knew he shouldn't be seated at that moment in the oversized, leather theatre chair in her home eating cheesecake. He'd promised to be a gentleman as well as not cross the line of starting something meaningful with her considering he would only be in Atlanta for a few more months. Who knew where life would take him afterward for he was always jetting off to another country and sometimes with only a few hours' notice. His heart cringed at the notion of having to leave Harper. For the first time, he'd begun to feel at peace in his life. Perhaps Cannon was right—maybe it was time to settle in one place. And while he'd just met her, Hunter wanted to see where their relationship could go. She wasn't a one-night stand or fling kind of a woman, otherwise he wouldn't be sitting there watching the third quarter of a basketball game. Instead, he would've followed her through the sliding door of her bedroom and tore the red dress off of her.

"Hey, beautiful one."

Carrying two bottled waters, Harper plopped into the seat next to him and sat the bottles in the cup holder of each chair. She curled her feet under her and turned toward him.

"Hey, yourself. I see you found the remote control."

"Yep ... I'm a man. We'll find it quick. I can turn to something else if you're not into sports."

"Nonsense, I love basketball and my favorite player is on the court." She swiped the saucer with her cookies and cream cheesecake from the TV tray stand and let out the reclining part of her chair. "You better turn that up. I'm not a girlie girl who despises sports. I know how to hang with the fellas, too. I grew up watching and going to the games with my dad and my brothers."

"Cool. My kind of woman."

"Thank you. There's beer in the mini fridge behind the bar," she offered, pointing to the bar area behind the three rows of theatre chairs. "There's also top shelf alcohol for when my dad or brothers stop by. Help yourself to whatever you want."

A sly grin crossed his face. "All right, woman. Don't tempt me to pull you on my lap and finish what we started."

Chuckling, she shook her head. "Your toffee cheesecake will have to suffice ... for now."

For the next hour, they watched and cheered for their teams. He was pleased that she wasn't one of those women who watched the game just to see sweaty, hot men run up and down the court. She actually knew what was going on, yelled and cursed at the flat screen more than him, and drank her beer from a bottle. She was so into the game that at one point he swore she'd forgotten he was in the room.

Once it was over and her team won, she did a victory dance. "In your face, boo." Laughing, she crashed into her chair and took a swig of her beer. "I told you my team would win."

"Yeah, whatever," he grumbled, slightly aggravated that he'd lost a friendly wager with his brother Chase. "My team will make it to the playoffs."

"If you say so. I say not likely." She grabbed the remote from his lap and changed to the sports channel. "*Sports Fanatic* is on. Have to see what Rasheed Vincent's hilarious comments about tonight's game are going to be. The man is a riot."

"He's married to my cousin Bria, and yes, he's funny at all times. I think he missed his calling as a comedian."

"Really? He's your cousin-in-law? Oh, wow. He's one of my favorite basketball players. I hated when he hurt his knee for the second time and made the choice to retire. He still had some good years left."

"He's one of the greatest."

Yawning, she leaned back in her chair and stretched the recliner out. Her yawn caused him to do the same.

"Tired?" she asked in a sleepy tone.

"Nah, I'm good." He leaned back in his chair to raise the recliner part up and propped his feet on it.

"Me too," she said, followed by another yawn and relaxed her head on his shoulder.

*****

Harper sat up and stretched her arms out. The light from the flat screen that was on mute blinded her, and for a moment she had to remember where she was. Glancing around, she remembered she was in the media room and upon turning her head to the left, she spotted Hunter lying in the chair next to her sound asleep with a light snore. Normally, snoring bothered her, but his was more of a peaceful one. She had no idea what time it was and since the media room used to be a walk-in closet and bathroom in one of lofts she'd converted, there were no windows.

Letting the recliner down quietly so as to not disturb Hunter, she lay the blanket that rested on the back of his chair over him and tiptoed out of the room. Closing the door back softly, she trekked down the hallway until she made it back to the living area and saw the sun shining through the huge wall to floor window. Turning toward the kitchen, she discovered the clock on the microwave read 7:30 a.m. She contemplated waking him up or letting him rest, but she had no idea what time he had to be at work.

Normally this would be her time to work out, followed by a light breakfast, perhaps go back to sleep, run some errands, followed by another nap and then go to work at four in the afternoon. Even though lately she'd found herself going in earlier than necessary to work on upcoming events or take meetings with potential clients or their managers if they were a celebrity. While her three event planners performed their jobs exceptionally well, Harper had become somewhat of a micro manager for the past year or so and she wasn't even sure why.

London's reminder of their motto began to sound in Harper's head once more. Had she really been working hard without playing hard?

Sometimes work to her was playing hard because she loved the thrill and the atmosphere of the club. The joy of creating a fantasy environment for the patrons and the VIP guests was magic to her. Whatever they wanted, she could make it happen—within reason—and that alone made her job all the more exciting.

It had been her life for as long as she could remember having worked under her mother for almost a decade before the triplets took over. They'd made changes including changing the name from Zenith to Club Masquerade. They renovated the entire club and changed the laid back atmosphere to a more posh, upscale one that catered to the grown and sexy crowd. They'd added a full-service kitchen, and while they'd had private events before, the ones now were celebrity fueled ones which drew large crowds every night.

Spending time with Hunter had caused her to see her life in a different light. It had become the same mundane routine, and she'd become complacent with it. Like right now, today's original and usual agenda was on her mind but going into work early wasn't even necessary. Though yesterday she'd jotted down 'sit in on Shannon's noon meeting with DJ Scoop to go over his upcoming listening party'. But why? It wasn't her event or client. Harper trusted all three of the assistant event planners like she trusted herself, otherwise she wouldn't have hired them because she was a stickler for perfection.

"Good morning, beautiful," a groggy yet sensual voice spoke behind her.

Turning around she met Hunter's gaze and smiled as she reached to open the refrigerator.

"Can you stay for breakfast?" she asked.

"I can stay for as long as you want me to," he answered, stepping into the kitchen and snatching her into his nestling embrace. He laid a tender kiss to her forehead.

She giggled and normally would curse herself out for giggling like a silly teenager over a man, but she didn't care. No man had ever made her feel like Hunter did, especially considering going to the club early was the furthest thing from her mind.

"What time do you have to be at work?" She slid back to the refrigerator and pulled out ingredients for an omelet and croissants for French toast.

"I pretty much make my own schedule when I'm in the States. I have a conference call but it's later on this afternoon. What time do you have to be at the club?"

"Um … four o'clock," she replied, trying to remember her actual scheduled time. "I need to make a quick phone call to Shannon." She grabbed her cell phone that was plugged in on the island. "I'll be right back to make breakfast."

"Cool. I'll start the coffee," he volunteered, opening the bag of Sinful Delight sitting next to the coffee maker. "Maybe after breakfast you can show me around downtown some more, but after I go back to my hotel for a quick shower."

"That sounds like a plan." After kissing him on his cheek, she pivoted toward her bedroom with a huge smile on her face.

*****

For the next month, Harper continued wearing the huge smile as she showed Hunter all that Atlanta had to offer. The Centennial Olympic Park, Six Flags, plays and shows at the Fox Theatre, an Atlanta Hawk's game, Sunday brunch at Ray's on the River, and The Georgia Aquarium were all activities they'd managed to squeeze in around their work schedules. For once, she stayed away from the club on her off days and went in at her scheduled time. Of course this shocked her brothers and the staff, but she desired to savor every moment that she could with Hunter.

Today was no exception. While swinging hands with him, they strolled the grounds of the Atlanta Botanical Gardens, which was one of her favorite places to visit twice a year—or more depending upon the exhibits. It was also the venue she wanted for her wedding if that ever happened. Although it was something she envisioned in her future, a husband and kids seemed so far down the line. However, she admired her parents' love and adoration for each and hoped to have a husband who would gaze at her like her father would at her mother … with pure love in his eyes. Sometimes, she caught Hunter staring at her absently in the same way and while she loved it, at the same time it scared her. They never discussed the fact that he wouldn't be in Atlanta forever, but it was the elephant in their space. During their time together, they'd had plenty of passionate kissing sessions but the thought of going any further was something she didn't want to explore. Well, that wasn't true but Harper knew she'd become even more attached and would have a hard time letting him go if they shared a passionate night. So far he'd been respectful and hadn't pushed the issue, but she knew it was hard for him as well.

"Let's stop and take pictures in front of the fountain in the rose garden," he suggested.

"Perfect. It's one of my favorite places here. It's so tranquil. I remember the last time I came I sat on one of the benches and relaxed. Well ... I was making phone calls for work but at least I had a beautiful view."

"Mmm, like the one in front of me."

Heat rose to her cheeks and the smile she tried to suppress appeared. "You're so sweet." Reaching her hand up to his cheek, she blushed again as he kissed each finger tenderly. "I'm going to miss you when you leave."

The words that had been on the tip of her tongue finally spilled out. She wasn't supposed to tell him. That statement was to never leak from her mouth.

A sincere smile reached his face and Hunter kissed her hand once more before bending down and kissing her gently on the lips. "I'm going to miss you, too," he whispered. "Very much. I know we just met but I'm so into you, woman, I honestly don't know how I'm going to leave when its time. Hell, I'm going to Memphis the week after next, and I don't want to leave you for even a few days."

"It will be good practice," she said, as her voice cracked and her pulse raced faster than a greyhound sprinting to win the race. She slid from his embrace when she felt a tear wanting to emerge. Silently chastising herself, Harper pivoted toward the sidewalk that led to the fountain. "Let's take those pictures." Walking to the fountain, she sat on the concrete that surrounded it and bestowed a pretty smile on him.

He gave a knowing nod, and her heart skipped a few beats before hammering against her chest. She couldn't and wouldn't get that deep with him. While he was away in Memphis, it would prepare her for what life would be like without him in it. The more she told herself that ridiculous idea the more it saddened her, but she continued to flash smiles and change poses as he took the pictures.

After the photo session they made their way to the orchid conservatory but chose to sit outside on a bench while a field trip with middle school aged children ventured inside.

"This has been a beautiful day," she said, followed by a long sigh as she checked her watch. "I have to be at work in two hours."

"Still can't believe you're going in later than you normally do."

"Neither can my staff, but I'm sure they're secretly happy when I'm not around. I can be somewhat strict according to the whispers I've heard."

"You're a sweetheart. There's not a mean bone anywhere in your body."

"Well, I don't consider myself mean, but as a woman who owns a nightclub in a world full of men club owners, I have to be firm and assertive. I can't let anyone think that I'm naïve and don't know what the hell I'm doing. My mother was like that. I studied her over the years working at the club. She's tiny in stature and innocent looking like me, but trust me she's no pushover and the employees respected her. Now when she visits, they're all ecstatic to see her and treat her like a queen."

"That's understandable. I've watched you at work. You run a tight ship."

"Thank you. And I'm rarely worried when I'm not there."

"So your best friend is arriving the day after tomorrow?" he asked, taking a swig of his bottled water left over from their lunch at Lintons, a restaurant on the premises of the gardens.

"Yes, and I'm glad she's finally moving back to Atlanta. We're pretty much the only family she has. She doesn't have close friends like me in Charlotte, and since her ex-boyfriend at one point stalked her, I think its best that she's here among people who love her. Plus, I kind of want her and Mase together. I know that sounds crazy and I'm by no means a matchmaker, but I've always sensed they've liked each other more than they cared to admit."

"So what are you going to do?"

"Sit back and watch. Oh, and then there's Cam. He recently became serious with a lady named Simone. I swear she's the only woman I've ever liked for him, and I really hope things work out. It's obvious how much they love each other. "

"Seems like the Bennett triplets are all making love connections at the same time."

"You're silly," she said nervously, brushing off his comment. There could be no love connection between them. *This Bennett is having some fun.* "Since the weather is warmer in the evening, how about you come over tomorrow night for dinner? We can eat on the rooftop among the city lights."

"That's a wonderful idea. I'll bring the wine you loved so much from Café Intermezzo."

"Perfect. You know me well because I was going to suggest it."

"And the cheesecake?"

"Nope. I already made it."

"Really? All right, woman. You're going to make it very hard for me to leave in a few months."

A heaviness rose in her chest as she turned away briefly and realized for the first time that she wished he never would.

Chapter Six

Harper lit white tea light candles that she'd set around the terrace for her romantic dinner with Hunter. The night sky glistened with stars and the full moon was the perfect spotlight on the dining table for two. It was the ideal setting for tonight. She'd buzzed him up a minute ago and had just enough time to finish the ambience. Grabbing the remote from the table, she turned on her iPhone deck to a jazz playlist the DJ created for the club when they hosted the occasional Sunday brunch.

Dinner was done and waited under two warmer domes she'd borrowed from the club's kitchen. Smoothing down her black, strapless dress, she stepped into her heels and turned when she heard the door to the terrace open. Hunter emerged carrying a wine bag and a bouquet of pink and white peonies.

"Good evening, beautiful one."

"Good evening, handsome one," she greeted. "You're on time as always."

He halted, somewhat taken aback, and gazed around the area with a sexy grin on his face. It was his first time up there and she wanted everything perfect. A table for two covered in white tulle held their meal, along with wine glasses and a tall lit candle in the middle. To the left of it was a seating area with an outdoor wicker couch, loveseat, and table which sat under a pergola with outdoor white sheers. On the right side was a hot tub and Harper noticed his eyes linger there for a moment longer while wearing a sinful smirk. In the corner was an outdoor daybed covered with comfy pillows under another pergola which had ivy vines she'd trained to grow around it.

Chuckling, he shook his head as he approached her. "Soooo, is that where the magic happens?" he asked in a teasing manner, jerking his head in the direction of the outdoor bed. He handed her the flowers and landed an affectionate kiss on her lips.

"Mmm ... thank you for the peonies." After taking his hand and leading him to the table, she set the flowers in the middle as he pulled out her chair. "Honestly, I come out here to relax and read with a glass of wine. I have the occasional party with close friends, but this is my first time I've had dinner with a man. I guess you're special."

Leaning over, he dropped a sensual kiss to the back of her neck. "Love your hair pulled up in a bun. Easy access to your tempting skin." He placed a kiss on her shoulder followed by a soft bite to her neck.

"Mmm," she sighed as his lips warmed her skin. "I'll do it more often." She handed him the corkscrew next to her wine glass. "Filler up ... no, wait. Not too much for me. I'll have the giggles all night."

Hunter opened the wine, poured it into their glasses, and then topped hers with a villainous laugh. "I like your giddy giggles. Leads to me kissing your enticing lips and its usually without the wine."

"All right, now. Let's eat before the food gets cold." *And I lead you over to the outdoor bed for more than just kissing. But that can't happen. It can't.*

He sat in his chair and lifted the lid on the plate at the same time as she did. "Wow, this looks and smells delicious, beautiful one."

Requesting the recipe from Cameron—who was a master chef in the kitchen—she'd cooked rack of lamb, sautéed green beans with almonds in a garlic butter, and roasted-creamed new potatoes.

"There's plenty more in the kitchen along with your toffee cheesecake in the fridge."

Raising his wine glass in the air, he leaned toward her and clinked her glass. "My compliments to the lovely chef. Thank you for the home-cooked meal. It's one of the things I miss when traveling."

"I'm sure it is."

"You don't want me to leave, do you?" he joked, taking a bite of the green beans. "These are good. You keep cooking like this and I may not." He took a bite of his potatoes and nodded his head. "Oh, yeah. You are definitely trying to tie a brother down."

Harper laughed as she cut into the meat, but the truth was she didn't want him to leave. She was just getting to know Hunter and liked him way more than she should, but soon he'd be gone. She'd promised herself not to harp on it because she knew the circumstances going in. However, it didn't make it any easier.

*****

Hunter noticed the silence and melancholy that was wrapped around Harper that evening. Usually she was talkative and cheery, but tonight a solemn mood surrounded her and he sensed it was because he'd mentioned leaving. A part of him didn't want to either— the part that wanted to take Cannon up on his job offer as the director of the US headquarters just to be with Harper.

She was the epitome of what he dreamt of in the woman he wanted to spend the rest of his life with. Yes, she was beautiful, but outside beauty faded and he was more impressed with her overall personality. Her confidence, intelligence, and sassy wit along with the elegance and class that exuded from her no matter what were the characteristics that he admired. He loved the humbleness that she possessed and her independent nature. It was one of the first things that drew him to her.

Once they were finished with dinner, Hunter stood and reached his hand out to her.

"Dance with me," he requested as the jazz version of "Spend my Life with You" began to sound through the speakers. He'd loved the song ever since hearing it at Cannon's wedding a couple of years back. It was something about the words of the song that fit the way he felt about Harper and that shook him to his core.

Taking his hand, Harper stood and fell into his arms with a deep sigh. He nuzzled his head in her neck and hummed the song in her ear. She swayed in his arms and squeezed his shoulder when he began to place light kisses on the side of her neck. Angelic moans sounded from her throat, and she squeezed his shoulder again, sending an electric current to bolt through him. The willpower he'd been able to keep in check faded away with every tantalizing moan she uttered. Her hand sensually travelled up his cheek to his head and back down to his lips. She was silent but the insatiable expression on her face screamed at him loud and clear. Lowering his head, he touched her lips with his but didn't kiss her. Instead, they stared at each other with unwavering eyes until hers fluttered shut, and she kissed him as if she'd never see him again. Unwavering emotion poured over him at that thought and seized his heart in an uncomfortable imprisonment.

Hunter returned the kiss in a slow but unruly way, eliciting the most breathtaking sounds from her. Lifting Harper in his arms, he carried her to the bed and laid her down. Her fiery eyes turned dark with lust, and he knew what she desired. Sliding on top of her, she reached up and captured his lips as satisfied, relieved sighs escaped from her. Her body trembled under him as she wrapped her legs around his waist and kicked the heels off her feet. His manhood pressed against her center and the slight grind of her hips made it hard for him to turn her down. He wanted to be strong, but Harper evoked emotions on him that couldn't be turned off.

Lifting his head, he gazed down at her and ran a finger along her soft cheek. "Tell me what you want, Harp."

"A passionate night with you. No strings. No worries about tomorrow. Just us, right now."

"Glad I came prepared."

"So did I. I've wanted you from the moment I first saw you. Of course I have to admit it was more in a lustful way but now that I know the kind of man you are, I need to experience being one with you, considering I can't have you forever."

The thought of forever surged an uncontrollable shiver to bolt through his body and a guttural groan emerged at the thought of Harper yearning for him all this time. Yanking her up, he kissed her in a possessive manner as if she was all his and no one could ever have her again. He wanted to brand her and etch tattoos all over heart to make it clear she was all his. He had no idea where that notion came from, but his goal was to erase any trace of any other man she'd been with and replace it with the desire and craving for only him.

Sliding up the hem of her dress, Hunter travelled his hand between her thighs and a devilish grin bestowed on her face when he touched skin and not material.

"You're not wearing any panties," he murmured, sliding a finger inside of her as her back arched off of the bed.

"Mmm … um … I had a feeling I wouldn't … damn … need them." She could barely speak as he slowly slid in and out of her. "It feels so effing good, babe."

He loved the amorous expressions on her face that he placed there and the moans which amplified as he increased the speed. She clutched his shoulders and her head fell back against the pillows when he ran his tongue along her neck. She was exquisite. Passionate. Sexy. He didn't know how much longer he could hold out especially when his erection pressed so taut against his pants he knew it would burst through the zipper. The warmth and slickness of her clenching and grasping around his finger sent an electric current through him.

Sitting her up, he reached around to the back of the dress to unzip it but couldn't. "How on earth do you take this off? I really hate to rip it."

Rising off the bed, Harper stood and turned her back to him. "The zipper is at the bottom."

"Oh, that's different."

Kneeling behind her, Hunter began to drag the zipper up placing kisses along her back, shoulders, and neck until the dress fell off. Running his hands around to her breasts, he massaged them in a circular motion. Sultry purrs elicited from her and she turned her head slightly to reach up to his lips. He delved deep into her mouth and a feral wave of pleasure shook through him. Turning her around to him, he immediately sunk his mouth over one nipple while massaging the other.

"Mmm ... Hunter, that's perfect. Keep it just like that."

And he obliged as he nibbled and licked on her breasts back and forth like a starving untamed lion that hadn't eaten in days. The more she moaned and groaned his name, the more he sucked harder to hear the breathtaking sonata that he'd educed from her.

"I need you," she groaned, gliding her hand down to his pants and unbuckling the belt followed by the zipper. "Right now. I think we've done enough foreplay this past month." Reaching into his boxers, she ran her hand up and down his penis. "Don't you?" She rustled her other hand in his back pocket, pulled out his wallet, found two gold packets, and tossed them on the bed.

Instead of answering her, he stripped himself of his clothes quickly as she watched on in amusement. Standing in front of him, she traced a finger along his abs and up to his chest where she placed a kiss in the center.

"Mmm … I love chocolate." She licked around his nipples as he began to undo the bun on the top of her head until her hair fell around her shoulders. "Definitely an aphrodisiac. I literally can't get enough of you, but I need you inside of me."

Backing them up to the bed, he lightly pushed her on it and joined her. Swiping one of the condom packs, he secured himself. "Why not do both at the same time?" He centered his arousal over the spot where she craved for him to enter. As he teased it along the opening, she devoured the side of his neck like a starved animal. Pleasure raced in his veins and the groans that arose from him were unfamiliar and uncontrollable. Sliding inside of her slowly, he was engulfed in her warmth and the essence of what made her a woman.

She shifted under him and let out a long sigh as he began with slow, steady thrusts. He didn't know—and didn't want to know—the last time she'd had sex, but it was clear he was in unclaimed territory the farther he pushed inside of her. Her walls clenched around him as her hips began to meet his rhythm, and her pleased moans of ecstasy filled the night air and his ears with delight. Being one with Harper charged his soul and heart.

"What have you done to me, woman?" he asked in an intoxicating tone. "I've wanted to be one with you since the very moment we met. I haven't been able to concentrate without thinking about when I'm going to finally have a chance to make love to you."

"Me either, baby," she moaned.

His thrusts became deeper and more pronounced. His lips sought hers in a voracious kiss that didn't have any restraints or rules. Sensations of pure bliss pulsed through his body as she released loud cries of pleasure. He'd never wanted a woman as much as he needed and craved Harper Bennett. He couldn't get enough of his beautiful one. The way he fit with her perfectly as if he was molded from her canal and no one else belonged with her but him. A tiny wave of jealousy coursed through him at the thought that he hadn't been the only one. However, they weren't him and she'd never remember their names or faces once the night was over.

Witnessing her exasperated purrs set his body aflame, making him need her even more. He'd wanted to take his time, but the deeper they kissed the more she met his strokes in perfect sync. He loved the way she was in semi-control, making love to him back by purposely constricting around him and thrusting up until he couldn't move at all.

He slid out of her—much to her dismay, judging by the frown on her face—but he wanted to explore other parts of her body. Travelling his tongue along her blazing skin, he familiarized himself with her sensual curves, the beauty mark an inch under her right breast, and the cute little belly button that led to her center. He licked his tongue around her clit as her legs shook and he delved in between her folds to taste the sweet juice that she'd created thanks to him.

Harper's hands grasped either side of his head as he continued to lick and tease her. She giggled a few times, probably because of his beard growing in, but then let out a long wail when she jerked and trembled. As she came, her hips rose from the bed, but he held her firmly in place. Finally, he made his way back to her swan-like throat, which had produced all of the passionate cries that caused scorching flames to ignite in every cell in his body.

Hunter couldn't believe the effect Harper had on him in such a short of amount of time. Women didn't unhinge him because it had always been the other way around. But she was different and caused him to lose the control he thought he possessed.

"Come here," she whispered.

Her breathing had settled back down to normal but he aimed to change that. Picking her up off the bed, he stood and positioned her legs over the bend of his elbows while he clutched her butt. "Hold onto to me," he demanded. "Around my neck."

She giggled nervously. "Please don't drop me."

"Babe, you're as light as a feather. I got you. It will be like bench pressing."

He eased her down over his erection as a relieved moan escaped her throat. Her head fell back, and she gripped him tighter around the neck.

"Ah ... shit, Hunter. You feel wonderful."

"Lift your head and look at me. I need to see your beautiful face."

She obliged and settled her forehead on his. "Mmm ... um ... I can't ... breathe. It feels so effing good. Yes, big daddy ... don't you ever put me down."

The muscles of her walls constricted around him as he bounced her up and down while he stood in one spot. The more she dug her fingers into his skin, cursed, and screamed his name, the more he increased the tempo and grabbed her bottom even harder. Her sex-driven moans were unraveling him fast, so he walked her over to the bed and laid her down, never missing a beat. She settled her legs over his shoulders as he gripped her hands to the mattress.

His thrusts became erratic as his climax was near thanks to her, and he could no longer control his movements and actions. Her body vibrated with intensity as her orgasm released, pulsating around him, and he followed suit, slamming into her as curse words he rarely used ejected from him.

Hunter rested his forehead on hers while she cupped either side of his face. "Hey, beautiful."

"Hey, yourself."

Sliding off of her, he nestled her close in his arms as they both calmed their breathing down. The thought of being without her was no longer an option, and he vowed to make her his forever.

Chapter Seven

Harper rested her head on Hunter's bare chest with an exhausted smile on her face. They were sated after their intense lovemaking, but she wasn't too exhausted that she couldn't muster up enough strength for round two if need be. He'd energized and awakened a raw pleasure in her that was beyond anything she'd ever experienced with a man before. It wasn't awkward as some of her first times with past boyfriends. No, it was sensual. Emotional. Fervent. The instant connection that they'd shared upon meeting progressed even higher. She'd soared like an eagle high above the sky and wasn't ready to fall to the ground just yet. In fact, not at all.

A part of her was a tad saddened because this couldn't be her forever, but she didn't regret her decision. She was a grown woman with needs and at that moment that need was him. Normally, she would never have sex with a man after only knowing him for barely a month and no plans for a real committed relationship. However, their attraction to each other had started the first time their eyes met, which had never happened to her before.

Harper's curiosity had gotten the best of her, and now she was cocooned in his embrace, basking in an afterglow under the starlit night. She nearly giggled at the ironic fantasy. She'd read hundreds of romance novels in that very spot and had imagined herself with the hero making love to her under the stars. Now she was in the arms of her real-life-hero and didn't want it to end. *Ever.* Her heart clenched in pain, but she had to brush that away. Sadness couldn't prevail right now. She could cry once he left, but at the present, she'd enjoy his presence.

Stirring in his arms, Harper squeezed closer to him. "I hope we weren't too loud," she said. "I kinda forgot we were outside on the roof. But then again, who cares?"

Shrugging his shoulders, he let out a light chuckle. "Yeah ... I don't think either of us cared. Of course, when I heard the sirens I have to admit I did wonder if someone had called the cops on us," he teased, popping her bare butt.

"Ha! Me too. Do you think the news helicopter that flew by a few moments ago could see us?"

"Well, it did linger for a moment," Hunter replied with a sarcastic laugh. "Not that I blame them. You are one fine woman."

"Thanks, love."

Hunter kissed her forehead and pulled her closer. She snuggled to him when her mind brought her back to the fact that she couldn't become too comfortable. This was supposed to be a fun, temporary situation. *Um ... too late for that, Harper Elaine Bennett. You're now in deeper than you should be.* Sighing, she smashed even nearer, which was barely impossible. She was basically glued to him.

"Are you okay?" he asked, rubbing her back in a soothing, circular motion.

"Perfect."

"No, you tensed up. Are you having second thoughts?"

Sitting up immediately, she stared down at him and rested her hands on his chest. "Honestly? No. I've decided to just be carefree and spend every moment that I can with a wonderful man until he jets off once more to help make the world a little better. Then you'll forget all about me. You don't have to worry, though, I'll be fine. Plus, you'll be gone for a week visiting your family. I'll experience what it's like to not have you around for a while."

Even though she'd spoken the words, Harper knew it was a lie and the I-don't-believe-you expression on his face hinted at such.

"I see. First of all, I'm not going to forget about you. Second of all, who says this has to end when I leave?" He put his hand up in a halting suggestion. "And before you tell me you don't do long distance relationships anymore, I'm not him, Harper."

"I know you're not, but I'll always wonder in the back of my brain whether or not you're seeing someone. Heck, for all I know you could have a girlfriend or a wife and three children somewhere in Timbuktu." She laughed at her silly notion. "I know you don't, it's just better this way so I won't be sad ... or rather not *that* sad when you leave."

"You know I'm not giving up, right? We've been very honest with each other since day one." Cupping her chin, he kissed her softly. "This isn't a fling, and I think you know that or you would've never made love to me the way you did tonight."

Knowing there was truth in every word he'd stated, she nodded her head and whispered, "I'm scared, Hunter."

Smiling with sincerity, he gathered her in his arms once more. "There's nothing wrong with that, beautiful one."

"Goodness, I'm going to miss you calling me that."

He sighed deep and shook his head. "You'll never have to experience that."

Burying her head in his chest, she avoided eye contact with him as she tried to be strong. Yes, she'd heard the words come out of his mouth, but she needed to think realistically and rationally.

"You should travel with me to Memphis," he suggested. "My mother would adore you."

She froze for a moment as his suggestion soaked in. *Go to Memphis? Meet his mother?* However, the more she thought about it the more she kind of liked the idea.

Lifting her head, she sat all the way up and straddled him. "Mmm ... a vacation would be nice. I've never been to Memphis before."

"I guess it's hard for you to get away?"

"No. I have a ton of saved vacation time because I rarely take days off. However, I have the best event planning staff in the city so I'm not too worried about things going awry in my absence. Honestly, there are times when I'm not needed. Tell you what, if you're serious, I'll check the schedule for that week and let you know. There are two events that I'm over, but Shannon can handle those."

"That sounds like a plan. And yes, I'm serious. Very serious. I've already told my parents about you."

"Oh ... wow." Considering she hadn't mentioned him to her parents, she was sort of flabbergasted. The only reason her brothers knew she was dating him was because she finally had to tell them when Hunter began to spend more time at the club. And she had a sneaky feeling Mase had one of his hacker buddies research him. It wouldn't be the first time, and there were a few instances she'd been grateful for the information.

"You sound surprised."

"Well, you know men ... uh ... men don't ... I have brothers and if they aren't serious about a lady, our parents don't know they exist. Heck, half the time I don't know either unless the women pop up at the club. So, yes I was surprised, but I have to admit that's very sweet."

"Well, the times my mom has questioned if I'm seeing someone I've told her yes, but no one special. When she asked me last week I told her yes, and that Harper Bennett was the most amazing and classy woman I'd ever met. I told her how beautiful you are inside and out, and that you're the epitome of what I've searched the world for. I told her once my job here is complete, I can't see myself leaving you. It literally pains me to say that, Harper."

His words knocked the wind out of her, and the tears that wanted to roll down her cheeks earlier finally cascaded. Wiping them away, he sat up and kissed her tenderly.

"You're making it very hard to say no, Hunter."

Lifting her, he carried her over to the hot tub. "That's the idea." Walking up the three steps, he lowered them in the bubbling warm water and sat down with her straddling his lap.

"Are we taking a skinny dip?" she asked mischievously, circling her arms around his neck and glad she'd turned the hot tub on before he'd arrived. She felt the hardness of his manhood against her, and she knew the last thought in his brain was a skinny dip.

"No, we're going to make love again."

"I love your idea," she said, lowering her lips to his.

*****

Harper scanned the women's watches in the glass display case at the Tiffany and Co. store inside of Phipps Plaza. They were all gorgeous, and she couldn't decide which out of her three favorite ones to select for her mother for a Mother's Day gift.

"What do you two think?" she asked, pivoting around to her brothers. "I believe Mother will like the one with the roman numerals and the diamonds. Its elegant and sophisticated like her."

"Whatever you select," Cameron shrugged. "This is your specialty, you know."

"Yeah. You and Mom have similar tastes," Mason added. "I'm sure she'll love it."

Turning back toward the saleslady, she pointed to the watch in question. "Can we see this one, please?"

Smiling, the lady unlocked the case and handed the watch to Harper. "Here you go. Try it on."

"With pleasure," she replied, holding out the watch and her wrist to Cameron.

Cameron nodded with a pleased expression as he clasped the timepiece around his sister's wrist. "I think this is the one, too. It looks like something she'd wear."

"I agree," Mason answered, admiring the watch before strolling away with Cameron.

"Perfect." After unclasping it, she handed it back to the saleslady. "We'll take this one and as well as the pearl bracelet."

"Your mother is going to love these. I'll wrap everything beautifully for you, Ms. Bennett."

"Thank you," Harper stated, gazing around the store. Her brothers weren't much for shopping which was why she'd already made note of exactly the jewelry she'd intended to show them when she searched on the store's website the night before. Curious as to what they were pointing to, she walked over to where they stood and squeezed in between them which had been her favorite place to stand since they were children. She'd always felt extra protected between her brothers and was elated when Mason decided to work at the club so the trio could all be together once more.

Peering at the display case in front of them, Harper was quite astonished to witness her brothers perusing rings. *Women's rings.* They were both single even though she kind of hoped that would change for Cameron now that he was in a serious relationship with Simone. Plus, with the arrival of London a week ago, perhaps she and Mason would realize they were meant to be, as well.

"Soooooo … which one of y'all are getting engaged first?" she teased. "And when it happens I have to select the rings."

The brothers laughed a little too loud and Cameron answered her first. "We were commenting on the prices."

She smacked her lips and swished her mouth to the right. "Boy, bye. You can't be your usual thrifty self when you buy Simone's ring."

"Don't worry, I know," he answered as the trio strolled over to the cash register as the saleslady motioned to them. "Nothing but the best for her. When I buy a ring, it'll be the one time I don't care about how much something costs."

Mason slid his hand in his jeans' pockets and shook his head in the negative. "Yeah, and you know I'm not the marrying type."

Harper laughed at Mason's answer. "Whatever. Let's pay for this and then hang in the mall for a bit."

After grabbing coffee from Starbucks, Harper decided this would be the perfect time to tell them about her trip to Memphis next week. She figured since they were in public perhaps they wouldn't question her as much.

"Sooooo … I wish we could actually spend Mother's Day with Mom, but Dad is very excited about taking her to Niagara Falls and then on to New York City in the Winnebago."

Cameron nodded with a slight sigh. "I'm disappointed as well. She's going to miss the Mother's Day Sunday Jazz Brunch at the club this year."

"I hate that considering she started the event eons ago." Harper paused as she took a deep breath. "I'll be out of town next week, but I'll be back in time for the dinner party for her before they head out."

"Oh? Where will you be next week?" Cameron inquired, taking a sip of his coffee.

"Yeah, I don't remember you mentioning going out of town," Mason said, with a questionable stare.

Harper sensed the wheels in their heads churning, and she laughed nervously.

"Well, you two are always saying that I spend too much time at the club and that I never take my vacation time. So, I've spoken to Shannon and she's going to handle my usual tasks while I'm gone. Of course I'll only be a phone call away if she has any issues, but I'm sure everything will run smoothly. She did an awesome job when I was out for a week last winter with the flu."

Cameron halted in front of her and a curious grin rose up his jawline while Mason's forehead wrinkled as he tapped his chin.

"What?" she asked, eyeing them back and forth. *Oh boy. Here we go.*

"That's fine and all about taking your vacation time. You really need to, but … uh where are you going?" Cameron asked again.

Mason chimed in, "And with whom? Besides the family, you only travel with London and she's starting a new job."

Spotting a nearby bench, she beelined to it and plopped in the middle. She thought surely they'd sit on either side, but they didn't. Instead, they hovered over her as if they were about to interrogate her even though she assumed they'd already figured out who she was travelling with.

Sipping her coffee deep, she let the warmth of it soothe her before answering. "I'm going to Memphis with Hunter," she answered calmly even though her heart skipped a few beats. "You two know we're dating."

Cameron folded his arms across his chest followed by Mason. Even though the brothers were fraternal, they shared the same stances, curious facial expressions, and questioning eyes. And while they had different personalities and interests, the one thing they had in common was being overprotective of her.

Mason spoke first. "Didn't you just meet him?" he asked a little too sternly.

"And?" she asked with a shoulder shrug. "What's your point?"

"Why Memphis?"

"He's from there. We're visiting his family while he's in the States. I already told you both about his job with

Doctors Unlimited. And, Mason, don't stand there and act like you haven't had one of your buddies research Hunter. You probably have a dossier on him right now. Don't you?" she inquired, pursing her lips.

"Yep, my boy Wiz already handled that for me," Mason answered matter-of-factly and sipped his coffee.

"And apparently you didn't find anything alarming or you two would've already warned me and demanded I stop seeing him. It wouldn't be the first time."

"He seems like a cool guy," Cameron said sincerely. "We only want you happy, but we know your position on long distance relationships. I'm surprised you agreed to go out with him."

"Me too, but there's something about him I couldn't say no to. I decided to take a chance, follow my heart, and I'm glad I did. Honestly, I don't know what's going to happen in the future, but I've enjoyed being with Hunter. I think Dad will even like him. I know Mom will."

"Well, you've never made rushed decisions so I trust your judgment, Harp."

"Thank you, Cam. Mase, you're cool?"

"Yeah, but I need to know where you're staying in Memphis and the phone number."

"We're staying at The Peabody and the only number you need is mine and you have it."

"Well ... pick up if either one of us calls."

"I always do ... unless of course ... you know I'm occupied doing what grown folks do," she teased.

"Harp, we really don't need to know that," Mason said seriously, waving his hands in front of his face. "You're our baby sister." After tossing his coffee cup in the nearest garbage can, he reached into his pocket to pull out a gourmet lollipop.

"Um ... you do realize we're all the same age and none of us are virgins, right?" She loved joking with them in that way so they would drop the subject.

Cameron let out a frustrated sigh. "We're older by a few minutes, and we really don't want to know."

Rising, she stood between them and linked her arms around theirs. "Yeah, whatever. You two behave while I'm gone, and I'll try to do the same while I'm away." She laughed out loud and the brothers glanced at each other over her head, trying not to follow suit, but it was no use as the triplets all laughed the same hilarious laugh together.

*****

"I can't tell you how elated I am that you're finally back in Atlanta," Harper said to London as they began their five-mile walk and jog around the base of Stone Mountain. Their plan was to jog every other mile starting the first one with a fast walk with the goal to be finished in an hour before the park opened at ten.

"Me too. Atlanta has always been home, and of course being with you and your brothers."

"Well, we're all family and who knows? Maybe you'll be a Bennett one day," Harper said in a sing-song voice. "I can plan the wedding." She clapped her hand with her water bottle. "It's going to be epic."

London chuckled sarcastically and stretched her arms over her head. "Here we go again."

"Don't worry. I promise not to say anything else unless you ask for my advice."

"Thank you," London replied in her serious, news anchor tone which continued to the next topic. "Now let's talk about you and Hunter. He seems like a really nice guy. Aren't you glad I suggested you go out with him and have a little fun while he's here?"

"Yeah … but … I … kind of …" Harper breathed out and shook her head. "Arg!"

"What's wrong?"

"I've fallen for him. *Hard.* Like I can see myself with him and no one else. Like I want to be Mrs. Hunter Arrington."

"I can tell."

"How?"

"You're glowing and you agreed to go to Memphis with him to meet his family. That's a major step."

"Yes, but I don't know what I'm going to do with myself when he leaves. Thinking about it literally hurts my heart. Heck, I didn't miss what's-his-face at all, and I miss Hunter already."

"Half a mile mark," London stated, pointing to the flat, brass marker on the sidewalk. "Prepare to jog soon."

"Heck, I need to run off some of this frustration."

London's eyebrow rose along with a saucy grin. "Sexual frustration?"

"No, girl. He's perfect in that department. Too perfect. I almost wished he sucked, but I haven't been this sexually carefree and connected with a man before. *Ever*. When I see him or hear his voice over the phone, I literally want to make love to him. Our first time was such a passionate night. *All* night. The times since have been just as mind blowing, but it is so much more than sex. I feel connected to him in every aspect. Mentally, physically, spiritually, and emotionally all wrapped up in one big melting pot in our own universe."

"Okay … you've never spoken like that before. You're falling in love with him."

"Yes, and I've been trying my damnedest to ignore it but it's no use. And he keeps stating we don't have to stop seeing each other once he leaves, but …"

"The long distance scares you."

"Yes, and its more than the long distance. At least with what's-his-face, it was a two-hour flight to New York for a few days. Hunter will be in another country on another continent. That is not a weekend trip."

"Well, you'll earn a lot of frequent flier miles," London joked.

"I don't know if I'm going to continue seeing Hunter once he leaves."

"You're kidding, right?" London asked with a slight frown.

"No. I don't know," she shrugged, "I'm happy to be with him but terrified at the same time."

"Take it one day at a time. I know he has to travel for his job but perhaps that's only because it's just him. Hunter doesn't have anyone to be responsible for except himself. Who knows? Maybe he sees things differently now that he's met you and has stated he wants to continue the relationship even after he leaves. Apparently this isn't a fling for him. I've seen how he gazes at you. The man is smitten."

"Mmm … like Mase."

"Don't start," London said, playfully punching Harper's arm.

"I hear you, L. I need to make a decision." She looked ahead and spotted the next marker on the sidewalk. "Almost time."

Harper added a few lunges to her walk while sliding the scrunchie off her wrist to pull her hair into a ponytail on top of her head. As they passed the one-mile marker, the ladies began to jog at the same, steady pace. Harper let the tension go as she jogged and meditated while admiring the tranquil scenery of the trees and the lake. The outdoors had always been a refuge for her during times of frustration or just needing to escape the noise of the club world. It was one of the reasons she'd bought all three penthouse lofts so she wouldn't have to share the outdoor space.

"Whew!" London said as they passed the two-mile marker and the ladies began to walk again. "That was exhilarating. How do you feel?"

"Better." Harper took a swig of her water. "I'm a little nervous about meeting his parents, though. I can't believe we're leaving tomorrow morning."

"Mmm …" London answered with a mischievous expression.

Harper glanced at her from the corner of her eye. "Now look, don't be getting busy all over my house with my brother," Harper teased, waving her finger in the air. "I have cameras."

"Girl, stop. However, I may have to raid your closet." ·

"Knock yourself out."

London took a swig of her water. "Almost time to go again. You wanna jog for two miles?"

"Let's do it."

On their two-mile jog, Harper let London's words sink in about Hunter. Perhaps she was right. Hunter loved to travel because he didn't have any commitments and ties, besides his immediate family. While she didn't want to drive her hopes up, Harper decided to follow her best friend's advice and take it one day at time.

Chapter Eight

Harper fixed her hair in the mirror for the hundredth time. There was one curl that wouldn't behave and it threw off the look she desired. Sighing, she grabbed the curling iron once more and tried again. She rarely put heat in her hair herself once she left the salon, but desperate times called for desperate measures. She'd worn pin curls on the six-hour drive to Memphis and had expected her tresses to fall in place as always.

"Arg," she screamed out, dropping the iron onto the vanity when the strands still wouldn't curl in the direction she'd wanted. "Come on hair. Not today, dang it."

Strong hands encircled her waist from behind as Hunter placed a light kiss on her neck and caught her eyes in his in the mirror. For a moment all was well in her world as a tingle soared through her veins at his gesture.

"You're beautiful," he complimented, kissing her neck once more. "Your spirit is beautiful."

She smiled at his warm words. "That's sweet, but I want it to be perfect." She sighed deep and twirled the curl around her finger, but that didn't help either. "I'm meeting your family."

"You have nothing to worry about," he reassured, pulling her against him. "My family is going to love you."

"Goodness, I hope they do."

"They will. I've told them all about you and if we don't leave in ten minutes, we will be late for dinner and my mother hates tardiness."

"Yes, I remember you saying that," she replied, grabbing a hairpin to repin the curl. Sighing, she gazed over her outfit once more and hoped the wide-legged, off-white dress slacks with a green, ruffled blouse was conservative and classy enough to meet his parents. Opening her travel jewelry box, she picked out gold hoops and a gold necklace with a diamond heart charm. Hunter placed the necklace around her neck while she put the earrings on and then proceeded to turn off the curling iron.

"You look and smell lovely," he admired, inhaling the Si by Giorgio Armani perfume he'd given her for a "just because" gift.

"Thank you." Turning on her heel, she left the bathroom. "I think I've found a new fragrance."

Harper decided to no longer fret over her appearance and was quite surprised in her actions. She was never anxious about meeting the parents and usually looked forward to it, especially if she was in a serious relationship. However, because she didn't know where she and Hunter would wind up, she was overly antsy. She cared for him more than she should, and to her being introduced to the family meant something more than a random guy she was dating. The fact that he'd told his mom that she was special made her nervous. Harper knew Hunter wanted a relationship past him leaving, and she hated to admit to herself that her feelings matched his.

Hunter followed her out to the sitting area of their suite where she plopped in a chair and slid on her strappy, nude sandals. Kneeling in front of her, he buckled them for her.

"You know it's okay if you wear jeans like me," he reminded, running his eyes over her attire.

"I'd prefer to be comfortable but not for the first meeting. First impressions are lasting ones. Besides, I brought my black skinny jeans. Your favorite ones …"

A naughty smirk raised up his cheek. "I do love those. Sexy indeed. So, you're right. What you have on is perfect or I'd find myself squeezing your butt every chance I'd got."

"Exactly."

Her mind ran rampant with all the information he'd told her about his family on the drive to Tennessee, but Harper wanted to make sure she didn't fumble once she finally met them. "Okay, so your mother is an attorney specializing in criminal law, and we're in the same sorority so that's always a plus. Your father is a federal judge and they met at Yale Law School but both grew up in Memphis yet they didn't know each other. Your baby sister, Addison, is a wedding/event planner and preparing to move to St. Simons Island. Your other sister, Zoe, is away at Harvard Law School and Chase is an attorney as well."

"Yes, he's an assistant DA."

"Oh, right, and you two are nothing alike personality wise. Cool name though."

"Yeah. My uncle's wife's maiden name is Chase and my mother liked it."

"There's a Chase family in Atlanta."

"Yeah. That's Aunt Darla's side of the family. We're not blood related, but we still consider each other as cousins. I'm really close to Braxton, but I haven't had a chance to see him since he's on tour with his jazz band. But I had dinner with the rest of the family at his jazz and dinner club when I first arrived in Atlanta. We're all family."

"Small world. I don't know them on a personal level, but we run in the same circles." She inhaled as she became nervous once more. "Okay, what else do I need to know? Does anyone have any weird quirks? Do I need to call your father Judge Arrington? Is your baby sister going to look me up and down kind of how I do the chicks my brothers date? The ones I know I'm not going to like?"

Chuckling, he finished the buckle on the last shoe. "They will all love you," he reassured once more, kissing her forehead before standing them both up. He drew her against him and smiled sincerely. "Trust me, I don't bring women home just because. They all know you're very special to me. And no, my sister would never do that. Or at least not anymore. Calm down, beautiful one."

Sliding from him, Harper grabbed her purse from the seat cushion, slung the straps over her shoulder, and intertwined her fingers with his. Hunter squeezed her hand in a comforting manner as they walked toward the door, and she said a little prayer that the Arringtons would love her.

*****

Hunter opened the front door of his parents' home in the midtown area of Memphis with the key that he'd used ever since high school when his parents' had bought the vast property. He always kept the key because it reminded him that he had a home to go to. Even with all his travels and not having a true place of his own, his family's house was the one place he could call home. However, lately that had nagged him because a part of him yearned for a place to settle and put down his roots. Being with the lovely woman standing on the step behind him had caused Hunter to really think about his life in a different light. The notion of Harper not being with him tugged at his heart immensely.

He glanced back as she slid the hairpin out of her hair and slipped it in her purse. He mouthed "perfect" when the curl fell into place, and she let out a relieved sigh. She'd calmed down a tad in the short car ride from downtown, but he understood her nervousness. Giving her a reassuring kiss on the cheek, he let her pass through into the two-story foyer. The huge crystal chandelier sparkled as it always had, and the walnut hardwood floors were freshly polished. An oversized circular credenza stood in the middle and held family pictures from over the years. Everything was crisp and dust-free. His mom was a stickler for their home always being immaculately clean and had two maids to make sure of it.

Two staircases on each side met at the second floor landing where another chandelier sparkled bright in the hallway. His room was up there, and while he'd wanted to stay at the family estate, Hunter knew his mother would've put him and Harper in separate rooms. Sneaking down the hall could've worked except for the cameras his dad had installed a few years back.

Hunter hadn't been home in almost a year even though he'd seen his family a couple of times on vacation but a peace fell over him when he squeezed Harper's warm hand. The aromas of delicious home-cooked food filled the atmosphere, and he'd eaten light that day because he knew his mom would prepare all his favorites.

"Mmm ... smells like apple pie in here," Harper said, closing her eyes and inhaling the air.

"It is. It's my favorite. My mother makes it when I come home, along with homemade vanilla ice cream."

"Oh, I love her already. My dad used to make homemade ice cream for me and my brothers when we were children. Cam does it now."

A familiar cheerful laugh followed by the fast click of heels, and Hunter wasn't surprised to see his lovely, dainty mother running toward him from the dining room. He almost chuckled as she wore pearls around her neck, a flared purple dress with a matching cardigan that resembled something Michelle Obama would wear, heels, and an apron. She reminded him for a moment of June Cleaver who was always dressed up to vacuum the house before Wally and the Beaver made it home. Everything was topped off by a see-through hair bonnet that covered huge pin curls. His mind wandered back to Harper earlier as she fussed over her hair.

"My baby is home!" Evelyn Arrington exclaimed with a wide smile as her son picked her up for a hug. "Aww, look at you," she beamed, kissing his cheek when he placed her back on the floor. "I know we saw you a few months ago in Martha's Vineyard but family vacation isn't the same as being home."

"Yes, Mother. I agree." Smiling, Hunter wrapped his arm around Harper's waist. "Mother this is Harper Bennett."

"Nice to meet you, Mrs. Arrington," Harper greeted warmly, holding out her hand.

Evelyn smirked and shook her head. "Nonsense child. We're huggers," Mrs. Arrington stated, giving Harper a strong hug. "And please call me Ms. Eve. We're not that formal around here. Goodness, you're even more stunning than the pictures Hunter emailed me. You're absolutely breathtaking."

Harper's eyes grew wide as saucers as she peered at Hunter with a questioning smile. Realizing he'd forgotten to tell her he'd sent his parents the photos from the Atlanta Botanical Garden's outing, he chuckled slightly.

"Why thank you, and you're gorgeous as well," Harper complimented in a sweet manner. "Love your purple dress."

"Thank you. Love your green blouse, Soror." Ms. Eve paused, interlinking her hand with Harper's as an impressed smile crossed her face. "Now everyone is waiting for you two down in the media room. The basketball game will soon be on, so May and I made all kinds of sports event type foods, plus some of Hunter's favorite dishes. While I love all the good you do for the world, son, I hate you don't eat a home-cooked meal on a regular basis. Perhaps that will change one day." She winked. "I'm going to check on my apple pie and then run upstairs to finish my hair." She kissed Hunter's cheek once more before dashing through to the great room.

Grasping Harper's hand, he gazed down at her warmly. "See, I told you she'd adore you right away. The reason why I know she does is because she said to call her Ms. Eve. Usually it's Mrs. Arrington unless she really likes the person."

She exhaled a tad and ran her fingers through her hair. "Cool. I guess we should head downstairs and hope everyone else feels the same."

Moments later they arrived on the terrace level of the home and landed in the great room where the rest of his family sat in oversized theatre chairs with their attention focused on the basketball game that had just started. Everything was exactly as he remembered except for the huge flat screen on the wall.

Hunter cleared his throat and his siblings, along with his father, turned their heads toward him. "Can a brother have a little love before y'all become engrossed in the game?" he asked in a teasing manner.

"Hunter!" Addison rose from her spot and ran toward him with open arms for a hug. "You're home."

"What happened to all of your hair, Addi?" he questioned, perusing her short, pixie style. "I'm surprised you chopped it off."

Addison shrugged her shoulders with a laugh and rustled her fingers through her dark brown hair. "I wanted something different considering I'm moving where it's mostly sunny and warm year round. New life. New haircut." She paused and placed her cinnamon, doe eyes on Harper. "And you must be Harper. He can't stop talking about you whenever we've chatted lately." She grabbed Harper for a hug and graced a heartfelt smile upon her. "So glad to finally meet the special lady my big brother raves about."

"Nice to meet you as well, Addison."

Addison turned to Chase who'd approached along with their father. "Now if only my other big brother would find that someone special he'll stay out of my love life. They act like I'm a teenager and not twenty-three," she informed Harper followed by a playful punch to her brothers' upper arms.

"Girl, trust me. I understand your gripe. I'm the youngest of triplets and the only girl. My brothers swear we're not the same age."

"Exactly," Addison agreed. "I'm a grown woman and eventually they'll have to realize that."

All three men laughed at Addison for that would never happen as long as she was the baby sister. Hunter continued with the introductions before they all returned to the game. His mother soon joined them along with May, the estate manager and cook. The ladies set the food out on the table along with Harper and Addison assisting. Hunter caught his mom and sister exchanging happy smiles and nods while glancing at Harper. He knew they would adore her as much as he did. She was truly the one for him, and now that his family solidified that fact, he needed to convince her they were meant to be together.

During half time, Hunter decided to give Harper a tour of the house. They ended up in his old bedroom which is where he wanted to go in the first place. She strolled around the room and admired his Taekwondo trophies, baby pictures of him, and other mementos.

"You were an adorable baby," she said, pointing to a picture of him when he was six months old. "Look at those chubby cheeks."

"Thank you. I'm glad I grew out of them."

"Yes, because I love the chiseled look." She opened the double doors of his closet, which contained some winter clothes that he hadn't worn in almost two years.

Hunter perused the built in bookcase housing all of his precious souvenirs and artifacts he'd collected over the years. His mother had promised to keep them safe for him until he settled down and had a home of his own to display them. Each piece told a story about his travels—some good while others heart wrenching.

"Ever sneak a girl in here?" Harper asked slyly, sitting on the edge of the bed and crossing her legs.

"I plead the fifth," he chuckled, joining her and drawing her to his lap. "Nah. I got caught."

"Oh good," she joked, clapping her hands. "What happened?"

"The dog snitched on me. He barked so uncontrollably outside my door that my siblings and my parents rushed out to see what was wrong at two in the morning. My dad demanded I open the door, so I did. I wouldn't have gotten caught except that the girl in her attempt to hide in my closet had left a part of her dress sticking out. They wouldn't have noticed if it wasn't floral," he said, sarcastically. "I was grounded for a month. No car. No television. No extracurricular activities except for basketball."

"That's what you get," she teased, pinching his cheek.

"Look, I was only seventeen. Never did it again though. Well … not when they were in town."

"Goodness you're a mess."

He leaned them back on the bed and kissed her lightly. "And grown." Kissing her again, he delved his tongue deeper and wound it with hers in a slow, sensual dance. Clutching her hips, he drew her body hard against his and travelled his hand up to her breasts. Their tempo increased and the strain against his pants grinded against her.

She opened her eyes and pushed against his chest. "Boy, bye," she said, smacking her lips. "You know kissing me leads to other things. I have a rule. No hanky panky in the parents' home."

Sitting them up reluctantly, he scooted back. "Fine, but as soon as we're back at The Peabody …"

"It's on," she finished. "Hotel sex is hot because we have to be really quiet."

"Yes, and that's kind of hard for you to do." Tempted to kiss her again, he pulled her closer to him once more.

A knock on the ajar door jerked both their attentions to it with a nervous jump. Hunter thought for sure it was one of his parents, but it was Cannon wearing a mischievous grin.

"Excuse me for interrupting," Cannon began with a chuckle. "I was told you'd probably be upstairs."

Rising, Hunter trekked to his cousin and gave him a big hug. "Hey, man. Great to see you."

"You too. We talk and Skype all the time, but I haven't seen you in person in almost two years," Cannon stated, glancing over to Harper as she approached. "And you must be the lovely Harper. Heard a lot of wonderful things about you."

"Thank you," she replied, shaking Cannon's hand. "And the same about you and your beautiful family."

"Thank you. My wife and daughter are a blessing. They've changed my entire life."

Cannon beamed with delight at the mention of his family. Hunter was truly happy for his cousin and hoped to one day experience the same.

"I'm glad I have a chance to see you in person, Hunter," Cannon said. "Do you think you have a few moments to discuss Doctors Unlimited?"

Nodding, Hunter turned to Harper. "Is that okay with you, babe?"

"Certainly. I'm going to go grab another one of those Memphis Belle cocktails your sister made." She kissed Hunter on the cheek and walked toward the door. "That girl is a pro. I may need to convince her to work at Club Masquerade and not Precious Moments Event Planning."

"Come on, man," Hunter started once she left, "let's go down to Dad's study to chat."

"Sure, after I grab one of Addison's drinks."

"I agree, man. Me too."

Ten minutes later, they settled in Judge Arrington's rich wood-paneled study whose walls were lined with shelves and shelves of law books. The cousins shot the breeze for a bit until Cannon stopped laughing about one of their summer vacations to Martha's Vineyard and a serious expression washed over his features.

"I heard from the team in Ghana a few days ago, and they're ahead of schedule on building the medical facility. Dan stopped by there today on his way back to the States, and he said everything was progressing smoothly."

Hunter felt his heart drop out of his body, but he had to remain professional and composed. "Oh, I see. That's good." Normally, he would be ecstatic, and while he was happy for the organization, this meant his next mission was now a reality. Leaving Harper soon was now a reality.

Cannon tilted his head and tapped his chin. "I know we discussed you going there at the end of the summer but now it may be in the next month or so."

Hunter could barely hear the words as the annoying screech on the chalkboard sound scratched across his heart. He knew he would have to leave Atlanta, but he'd figured he had at least three more months to spend with Harper in order to convince her that they could still be together despite the distance.

"Hunter?"

Blinking his eyes, Hunter focused on his cousin who wore a bewildered expression. He had a feeling his face matched Cannon's.

Clearing his throat, Hunter took a gulp of his drink and was glad his baby sister made it extra strong after all. "No, I'm good. Surprised it was so soon. Do you know how long I'll have to be there?" He knew the answer to the question, but he'd hoped perhaps now it would change.

"Can't say. Maybe two to six months. Just until everyone is hired and everything is up and running efficiently like you've always done."

Hunter knew it would be closer to six months because that was the normal length. Sometimes he was in and out if he had to check on other facilities or there was an emergency somewhere, but for the most part four to six months.

"Cool. I'll start wrapping up things in Atlanta. The headquarters is almost complete. I have a few more positions to hire."

"Found a director yet?" Cannon asked, leaning back in the leather chair and shaking the ice around in his drink.

"I've met with a few candidates. Still dozens of resumes to sort through. A lot of qualified people are vying for the position. Some of them are already a part of Doctors Unlimited."

"I see. Are they as qualified as you? Offer still stands."

"I'm going to Ghana, remember? And then wherever else afterwards."

Releasing a half-smile, Cannon nodded in understanding. "Right. I know you love your current position. I thought maybe you'd at least give it some more thought, but I won't mention it again." Standing, Cannon walked over to Judge Arrington's desk. He browsed the family pictures for a moment before turning his attention back on Hunter. "Harper seems like a really wonderful woman."

"Yeah, she is. She's truly something special."

"Obviously. I can't remember the last time you brought someone home to Memphis."

"I had to. I wanted my mother to meet her."

"So you're going to do the long distance thing, huh?"

"That's my plan. Harper isn't onboard yet. She thinks I should continue my life as I always have but … I don't know, cuz. She has me thinking about things I've never considered before. I don't want to let her go because of distance. In my heart, I know she's the one."

Cannon raised his eyebrow and took a sip of his drink. "You know, I knew Yasmine was the one the second she let me go. I know that sounds weird, but she was willing to sacrifice our relationship for my dream." He chuckled sarcastically. "She told me to go save the world. It took me twelve years to get back to her. Sometimes I wonder how my life would have been if I hadn't left, but I guess there are too many what ifs. Not saying I regret creating Doctors Unlimited because I don't, but at the same time I had to spend over a decade without my true love. She says it was worth it, and she'd do it again. Me? I still question that at times. There had to be some other way to work it out. Nothing wrong with sacrificing but there's nothing wrong with compromising either."

"I hear you, big cuz."

"Think about what I said." Cannon shook the melting ice in his glass. "Let's go back to the game. I have a bet going on with Chase."

"Don't we all?" Hunter laughed but deep down he really didn't feel like laughing. Now he needed to muster up the strength to tell Harper he was leaving sooner than planned.

Hunter replayed his conversation in his head with Cannon later on as he finished watching the game with Harper snuggled close to him on the couch. They'd both known he wouldn't be in Atlanta forever. The words "sacrifice" and "compromise" rung loud in his ears. He'd found himself falling in love with Harper and the thought of being without her tore through his heart like a category five hurricane.

Chapter Nine

Harper rested her head on Hunter's shoulder as they rode the River Loop Trolley around downtown Memphis later that night before heading back to The Peabody. She'd had a wonderful time with his family and was relieved that they were as down-to-earth as Hunter. They'd made her feel at ease and welcomed into their home.

"I had a wonderful time tonight," she said, squeezing his hand.

"Me too … minus the fact that my team didn't win, and I had to pay my brother one-hundred bucks."

"And you keep saying your team is going to the playoffs. Not this year, boo."

"All right, perhaps not but I still had a wonderful time. Glad you were able to meet Zoe via Skype. My family really likes you."

"And I liked them. Your father is such a character with his funny-but-not-really-that-funny jokes."

"Oh, yes. We're all used to his silly jokes. People always assume he's some stuffy, old, snobbish judge but he's about the most down-to-earth, humble man you'd ever want to meet. My dad grew up in different times and not well off like we are now. He and his two brothers were from a poverty-stricken environment, but they'd made a promise to themselves to not let their environment hinder them from succeeding. Both have always remained humble and very much aware of the world around them. They passed those traits down to us. Once they lost their mother at a young age, my Uncle Francis—who is the oldest and sixteen at the time—helped my grandmother raise my dad and my Uncle Sean."

"I didn't know you had another uncle."

Taking a deep breath, he squeezed her hand. "Yeah, he went into the military after high school, but he was in quite a few wars and returned with PTSD. He committed suicide a few years later."

"Oh no. I'm so sorry. Did he have a family?"

"No, just us. I was really young when it happened. My cousin, Sean, who is named after our uncle, took it the hardest. He's a psychiatrist because of it and spends a lot of his time counseling veterans so they won't go down the same path. You'll meet him tomorrow night at my cousin's blues club on Beale Street."

"And your mother? Did she have a similar upbringing?"

"Complete opposite. Summers at her family's home in Martha's Vineyard, studies abroad, Jack and Jill events, debutante balls, et cetera. Both of her parents, as well as her paternal grandfather, were attorneys. She runs the family law firm now along with her brother and sister. Chase worked there at one point and I was expected to do the same, but after law school I began to work for Doctors Unlimited by accident. I was studying for the bar when Cannon asked me to look over some financial information for the organization considering that's my background. I passed the bar but decided I didn't want to practice. Mother understands, and Zoe is almost done with law school and looks forward to working with my mom."

"Do you think you'll always work for Doctors Unlimited?" she inquired as her voice cracked a tad, but she played it off by coughing.

He hesitated for a moment and drew her closer to him. "Mmm … that's a good question, Harp. That's always been the plan, but … as I grow older I start to see things in a different perspective."

Harper noted his hesitation and the strained expression that crossed his face while he spoke. Her female instincts kicked in, and though she wanted to turn them off, it was no use. The warnings had been there when he and Cannon had returned from their chat. Hunter had pulled her hard against him as if he needed to be comforted and was extra quiet which was totally out of character for him during a basketball game. But she couldn't let on that she was upset or disappointed. She knew in the beginning he would have to leave even though she was aware that he wanted to continue their relationship despite of the distance. Unfortunately, that wasn't going to happen regardless of the fact that she was falling in love with him.

Putting on a happy face, she beamed as best as possible to keep the tremors out of her voice. "Well, I think what you're doing is awesome. I can't wait for the fundraiser gala. A lot of people have RSVP'd."

"Good," he said with a slight nod. "I spoke to Cannon and the plans for the medical facility in Ghana are ahead of schedule. So I may be going there sooner than expected. Like in less than two months."

At that moment Harper's heart broke in a million pieces as the trolley stopped in front of their destination. She figured there was a change in plans but hearing it aloud made it real. Numbly, she stood and held his hand as they stepped off the trolley and onto the sidewalk.

"Wow. That was fast," she said, walking in front of him so he couldn't see the tears in her eyes.

"Yeah, but I'm not going to be there forever, Harp. Usually I'm off for a couple of weeks before going to check on another facility. I'll come back to Atlanta during those times. And while I'm in Ghana, I can come back and visit after a month or so for a few days."

"Stop, Hunter. That's a long flight and a lot of money for a few days."

He darted around and stood in front of her. Taking her hands, he kissed them and gripped them firm in his. "You're worth it. Besides, I have a huge trust fund that I received when I graduated from law school. I've barely touched it, so money isn't an issue. I finally have a purpose to spend it."

"Hunter, what if—"

"There's no what ifs. We will make this work. I told you in the beginning, this isn't a fling."

"Hunter, I know. But at the same time long distance scares me."

"You can always come visit me for a couple of weeks at a time … well, depending on where I am. Some places may not be safe. And I can do the same. I'm willing to compromise."

"I'm part-owner of Masquerade. I have responsibilities. I can't leave for weeks at a time."

"Your division seems to run fine with or without you."

"That's because I made it that way. Trust me, my crew is beyond trained."

"Exactly my point. Shannon hasn't called you at all, and you haven't called her because you know everything is fine."

"Why are you making this so hard?" she yelled. "You know how I feel about long distance relationships."

"No, why are *you* making it so hard? When two people care enough about each other they find a way to make it work despite the miles between them. I'm not the bastard that didn't appreciate you and apparently didn't love you. I know exactly what I have and what I want. And that's you."

"Babe, I don't want to be hurt again."

"I'm not going to do that," he said through clenched teeth.

Deep down she knew he spoke the truth, but at the same time she didn't want to ruin their trip by arguing in the middle of downtown.

"Hunter, let's have fun in Memphis this week and forget about what may or may not happen in the future. I knew you weren't going to be in Atlanta forever, and I've accepted that fact."

The strained expression returned once more to his ruggedly handsome face. Reaching her hand up to his cheek, she caressed it and stood on her tippy toes to lay a sweet, sensual kiss on his lips.

"I hear you, Hunter. I really do. Let's take this one day at a time." She kissed him again but this time more intense and deeper than before. His hands encircled her waist and pulled her hard against him. His kiss was possessive and made her feel as if she belonged only to him.

The giggles and catcalls from a few passersby reminded her they were standing on the sidewalk in front of their hotel. They both chuckled and pulled back a tad.

"I'm not giving up on us," he whispered against her lips. "But I'll drop it while we're on vacation. Besides, we have some unfinished business that started in my room at my parents' home."

"How about we take this upstairs?" she asked with a sultry smile, pulling him by the hand.

Once they made it to their suite, Harper barely placed her shoe inside before Hunter quickly shut the door with her against it. She thought he was going to kiss her, but instead he lingered his lips over hers and rested a heated gaze upon her face as he ran a sensual hand down to her pants and unfastened them. Twirling a finger around the band of her panties, he traveled it down the side of her thigh and slipped his hand inside her panties. Screeching out a loud, ecstatic gasp, she clutched his shoulders hoping it would help quiet her. However, he began to massage her center in a slow, deep, sensual motion that unraveled her even further and caused a long, passionate sigh.

An arrogant smile reached his lips. "Shh, baby. Don't you remember where we are?"

"Mmm …uh …" She clenched when he buried a finger inside of her. His eyes darkened as her lips parted and she tried her damnedest not to utter a sound. "Maybe you should … not go so de— I mean … maybe we should do things that won't … cause us … or rather me to be so noisy," she stammered, trying to stay upright against the door. She had no control over her body, but he did and was fully aware as he sped up the tempo.

"I can't promise that," he admitted through gritted teeth. "I love the beautiful, erotic emotions plastered on your face when you release a crescendo of sounds."

With his free hand, he gently grabbed all of her hair up and leaned her head back. Her eyes fluttered shut as he slipped another finger in, and the amorous moan she wanted to suppress flew out. His hot tongue scorched her neck in a ravishing kiss that turned harder with each passing moment. The willpower she wanted to possess apparently didn't make it into her suitcase when she'd packed for the trip because she couldn't find it anywhere in her to stay quiet.

Heat rushed over her body and her clothes constricted her. When she unfastened the top button of her blouse, he grabbed her hand and shook his head.

"Let me," he whispered, unbuttoning the blouse with one hand while the other one was still busy in her panties.

He held her stare, which was focused on his even as her knees began to buckle and Harper found herself sliding down the door, his smoldering eyes never leaving hers. The orgasm that was on the brink of releasing was near and when his tongue landed on the top of her cleavage, the moan she'd told herself to hold onto disobeyed as an orgasm tore through her body like an unexpected earthquake. She trembled and shook in his embrace, but he didn't let up as he unhooked her bra and tossed it somewhere on the floor. His mouth engulfed one of her breasts and then the other one, back and forth as charges of electricity continued to bolt through her over and over until she couldn't breathe and her vision turned into a blurry purple haze.

Settling his lips on top of hers, he muted her final cry out with a profound, savoring kiss which calmed her down a tad. The emotions and aftershock of shudders still migrated through her system. Standing back, he perused her for a moment while she leaned against the door trying to catch her breath.

She swiped her hand through her hair. "That was wonderful, Hunter."

"I'm not done. My addiction isn't satisfied yet."

"Well, come back over here," she demanded, stepping out her shoes and sliding her pants down to the floor. "I'll let you take off my panties."

He strolled over and yanked them down. "With pleasure," he said, dropping to his knees and immediately placing his tongue where his fingers had finished driving her insane.

This time she tried harder to hold in her ardent, arousing moans but once again this man was sending her on a feral roller coaster ride with vertical loops and 450 foot drops like the Kingda Ka coaster at Six Flags. Reaching behind her, she held onto the doorknob and draped her leg over his shoulder so she wouldn't fall off the magical intensity he created.

"Can't get enough of you, woman," he growled, raising her other leg over his shoulder and sliding her up until he stood with her sitting around his neck. His tongue never stopped licking and kissing her, causing the tremors from earlier to return in a raging fashion.

For a moment she was terrified out of her mind that he'd drop her, but he held her firmly in place while he groaned and feasted on her.

"It feels so good, Hunter."

"Tastes so good, too. I can do this all night. Mmm … delicious, babe."

"Goodness, I wish you could but I need you inside of me."

"Soon. Be patient, beautiful one."

"Mmm … please … oh … please, baby."

He continued licking and savoring her as the insatiable vibrations continued to wreak havoc on her. She found herself going in and out of an abyss of flames that had engulfed her skin. Harper tried to make a mental note of every single detail of their pleasurable rendezvous times so when he was gone she could remember how she felt. She hated the fact that this couldn't be her forever and hated even more that she was falling in love with a man who was the very personification of everything she'd ever desired in a soul mate.

Sliding her back down to the floor, Hunter scooped her in his arms and carried her to the bedroom.

"You're fully clothed," she said as he lay her on the comforter.

"Not for long." He raised his polo shirt over his head and unbuckled his jeans. Sliding them down along with his boxers, his hard erection sprung forward and pointed directly at her. "I guess he knows exactly what he wants."

Harper sat up and scooted over to the nightstand to retrieve a condom from the drawer. Tossing it to Hunter, he placed it on and joined her in the bed. Lifting her up, he flipped them so that she could straddle him. He clutched her hips and eased her down on him until he was snug inside of her. Immediately, she began to bounce hard on him and his contorted facial expressions signified he was in the same boat as she was a moment before. She decreased her tempo to a slow, sensual one, causing him to growl out in pleasure.

"Shit … woman," he yelled out through clenched teeth. "You're trying to get me back. Aren't you?" Grasping her breasts, he shook under her.

Snickering, she leaned over and kissed him, gliding her tongue inside his mouth in the same slow up and down rhythm on top of him. "Yes, you drove me crazy and now it's your turn to try and be quiet."

"Uh … shit … fucking shit, Harp. You are so wrong for this."

"I know," she whispered, sitting all the way up until he hit the spot inside that vibrated her legs and nearly caused her to fall off, but she had to stay focused. This round was all about him and making sure he never forgot this night.

Holding his hands down firmly on the mattress, she began to bounce up and down at a steady pace, sometimes switching to deep circles and then back to an unhurried tempo rising all the way off of him and then crashing back down. She continued the same pattern as his groans and cursing rose louder and the headboard repeatedly hammered against the wall.

Harper felt her own release near and tried to calm herself down as she rested her forehead on his. His hands clutched her butt and when he slapped it hard, she knew he was back in control again as he began to thrust upward off the bed into her continually until she climaxed once more.

"Did you really think I was going let you have all the fun driving me mad? Don't get me wrong, you did, but I never said I was finished with you."

Lifting her off of him, he rolled her over on her stomach. Clutching her hips, he pulled her back and that's when the hardness of him skated across her bottom. Hunter leaned over and kissed her followed by a cocky smirk.

"You may want to hold onto the pillow," he suggested with a wicked wink. "Tight. *Real* tight."

Before she even had time to do so, he entered her in one long stroke that caused her stomach to contract and a moan of pure pain and pleasure released from her. Clutching the pillow, he continued ramming in and out her at a speed and cadence that she couldn't define. It was passionate, awakening, downright erotic, and untamed all rolled into one. The ecstasy that ruptured inside coasted through her veins and soared her high into a fervent oblivion that she had no control over. The sounds escaping from her mouth mixed with the fireworks exploding around her sent Harper over the edge. She'd never experienced this much heightened sexual awareness with a man before. The connection of heart, body, and soul intermingled in sync as they were becoming truly one entity.

"You're mine," he growled, thrusting in out of her with long, deep strokes. "All mine. You hear me?"

"Yes, all yours," she breathed out. "All yours, Hunter."

He eased out of her and flipped her over on her back. Placing her legs around his waist, he entered her once more, but this time he kept still and stared down at her wearing a serious yet adoring expression. She shivered with anticipation as she slid her hands up his ripped hard chest and placed them on his shoulders so they'd be ready if she needed to grip when he started once more. Instead, he kissed her forehead and proceeded to kiss her lips in a sweet, unhurried kiss.

"Are you good, baby?" he asked, weaving his hands in her tresses and resting his palms on either side of her forehead.

She smiled faintly at his concern for her. "Perfect. I'm with you."

"I want to hold you for a moment."

"No problem. You can hold me as long as you need to."

"How about forever, beautiful one?"

"Forever would be perfect," she whispered as goose bumps tickled her damp skin and a shudder journeyed from the roots of her hair down to her pink painted toenails. Harper loved saying it out loud and her heart that was already beating erratically pumped even faster.

"I'm going to make that happen," he stated.

"Hunt—"

"Shh ... you trust me?"

"Yes," she answered honestly, for at that moment she really did believe they'd have forever.

"Then it will happen. I promise. We have lot of mottos in the Arrington family and one of them is have a little faith. I know you're the woman I'm meant to be with and that I will spend the rest of my life with despite distance or careers or whatever others obstacles are thrown our way."

Harper let the words sink in as he kissed her once more in the same unhurried fashion, as if time was on their side. It wasn't that she didn't have faith that everything would work itself out, but she had to think rationally—as always. That was her personal motto in order to not wind up hurt again in the end.

Hunter began to move inside of her, matching the identical pace of their tongues circling. This time her moans were softer and more emotional as he stroked in and out her in a slow yet deep and arousing momentum. The more he delved into her the more her heart raced like an Olympic track star crossing the finish line. The passion and emotional feelings for each other were intertwined just as their bodies were in perfect sync with each other. Tears flowed freely down her cheeks out of nowhere when they climaxed together and the way he kissed them away only made her more aware of how she never wanted to be without a loving man like him.

"I'm here, baby," he whispered.

"Sorry for the tears."

"No need to apologize. I understand."

"I don't want you to leave. I'm not ready."

"I don't want to leave you either, beautiful one."

Hunter turned them over to lie on their sides facing each other and he gathered her close to him. He rubbed her back in a comforting manner and kissed her forehead tenderly. Burying her head in his chest, Harper listened to his heartbeat as she made a mental note to remember the exact chords and music it created for future times when she'd be alone.

"Are you all right?" he asked, raising her chin to look at him.

"Yes, just a little stiff," she said with a light laugh and a sniff as the last of her tears had finally dried. She'd never cried during sex before but she couldn't help it. She was going to miss the hell out of him.

"Yeah, that was some workout. I guess you won't be going to the gym after all in the morning, huh?"

"Count me out. However, I still want to go down to the lobby and see the infamous Peabody ducks waddle from the elevator to their pond."

"Yes, it's cute for tourists. I think you'd enjoy it. Afterwards, The Civil Rights Museum, lunch at Rendezvous, dinner with my cousins, and then the casino in Mississippi the following day with Chase and Addison?"

"Yes. Can't wait to beat you in Black Jack."

"Care to make a wager on that?"

"Uh … didn't you lose to your brother tonight?"

"True, but I won with you," he said, squeezing her in his arms. "Everything will work out. I promise."

After a hot shower together, Harper snuggled in his secure, comforting embrace and watched the rerun of *Sports Fanatic* that they'd missed from earlier. She found herself drifting in and out of consciousness for it had been a long, exhausting yet fulfilling day. However, somewhere in her subconscious she heard Hunter whisper, "I love you, beautiful one," in her ear. Harper was too exhausted to spring her body up or jerk her head toward him especially considering the next thing she heard was a light snore. Perhaps, she'd misheard or was dreaming. She was dead tired and sated from their night of lovemaking yet she pressed her back harder against his chest and before her eyelids dropped for good she replied, "I love you, too."

Chapter Ten

Harper stood on the second floor overlooking the elite and wealthiest in Atlanta and other cities around the country mingling at the Doctors Unlimited fundraiser gala. She was quite impressed with the outcome of people on a Monday night, and even more elated that some of the ones who didn't show had sent checks to the organization. Though the club was closed to the public, it was packed as business as usual, and she hoped that the goal that was set would be surpassed.

She watched as Hunter moved around the room speaking to everyone and answering questions about the new medical facility in Atlanta. Every now and then she'd catch his gaze on her for a moment before going back to the business at hand. She was indeed proud of his accomplishments and all he'd done to help those in need. Even though he was leaving in less than a week, she'd tried not to focus on that and instead had enjoyed spending as much time as possible with him since their return from Memphis a month ago.

Waving at him when his eyes landed on her once again, she smiled wide as he excused himself from Cannon. They'd been in a deep conversation for the past five minutes and whatever they'd discussed had the cousins in a great mood as they departed. Perhaps they'd reached their goal or exceeded it.

Hunter made his way up the escalator to her. Harper loved that he had a habit of taking two steps at a time, his stare never leaving hers. It reminded her of when he'd spotted her at Wind Down Wednesday. She remembered being completely flustered that evening because she'd wanted Hunter more than any other man she'd ever been with. It scared her then and it scared it her now because the truth was Harper didn't know how she was going to cope once he left for Ghana and left her life. Even though she'd wrestled with the idea of the long distance relationship, she felt the best thing to do was to let him go. They could still communicate and be friends, but she didn't want the title of a relationship. She figured it would be less painful that way … yet every time she went over it in her head, an ache filled her heart and numbness swept over her.

"Hey, beautiful one. Why are you up here?"

"Watching to make sure everything is going smoothly. I was coming down to join you in a bit."

He drew her by the waist to him and placed a tempting kiss on her lips. "I need you near me. I'm leaving soon."

"I know," she whispered as her chest constricted and a wave of nausea hit her. "How's the fundraiser going?" She needed to change the subject to avoid turning on the waterworks in the middle of the club.

"We doubled the goal."

"Oh, baby, that's awesome."

"Yes, it is. Can we go to your office for a moment? I need to discuss something important with you."

"Of course."

Once there, she leaned against her desk as he stood in front of her. An eerie feeling washed over her and Harper had an inkling they were about to have the conversation she'd been avoiding. For the past month whenever he'd mention staying a couple despite him leaving, she would brush it off or change the subject. That wasn't going to be possible this time as his serious facial expression relayed.

"Great news. I spoke to Cannon a moment ago and there's a possibility that I won't be in Ghana for more than four months, plus—"

She glanced away momentarily before resting her eyes back on him. "Then off to another place for another four or more or less months. You don't know, and I can't live like that wondering when I'm going to see you again."

Closing his eyes, he ran his hands over his freshly shaven head and down his face before settling them on her shoulders with a comforting, sincere smile. "Babe, I keep telling you we'll be fine. I'm in this for the long run. What we have isn't a fly-by-night affair or meaningless fling. If that was the case, you would have never met my family, and I wouldn't be wrestling with the notion of being without you or making life changing decisions."

"I know, but I think that what we had was fun, and we should leave it at that. We can still keep in contact and hang out if you're ever in Atlanta again, but anything passed that …"

"Be quiet for a moment and let me finish." His forehead scrunched and he sighed deep. "Harp, Cannon has offered me the opportunity to be the director of the headquarters here in Atlanta. He's offered it to me several times in the past year and I've always said no. However, now I'm saying yes. I don't want to be without you. No more assignments. After Ghana, I'm back here. For good. *Forever* with you."

Harper exhaled while she soaked in his words as a pleased smile crossed her face. Was he really saying he would stay in Atlanta for her? Goodness, she wanted that more than anything but at the same time it was a huge sacrifice. What if they didn't work out after all? Would he regret his decision and blame her?

"Hunter, I don't want you to give up your life for me."

"Harp, I'm not giving up anything. I'll still work for Doctors Unlimited, but in a different capacity."

"When I first met you and I asked about your work with the organization, you went on and on about all your wonderful experiences helping people in need. I have to admit I Googled you after our first meeting, and read article after article about how you love making a difference. You did an interview with the Atlanta Newspaper about how you couldn't wait to jet off to your next destination. You've done so much for the organization and honestly it's one of the reasons why I fell so hard for you so fast because of your compassionate and unwavering spirit. Doctors Unlimited needs you in the capacity that you're in."

"Harper, will you listen to me for a moment …" He closed the gap between them and pulled her toward him, but she slid out of his embrace and scooted to the other side of the desk.

She held her hand up. "Wait. Let me finish. As much as I would love for you to be here with me, I can't ask you to give up your true calling. You'll be nothing but a suit working a nine-to-five at a desk. That's not you. You have this amazing spark in your eye when you discuss opening new clinics in third world countries that need medical care."

He met her behind the desk and cupped her chin. "Now I have a spark in my heart because of you," he said sincerely. "I love you, beautiful one, very much, and I know you feel the same way. I heard you that first night in Memphis before we both passed out."

She let out a deep sigh and the silent tears she wanted to keep locked away rolled down her face. The more he wiped and kissed them, the more they cascaded down. But she needed to be strong.

"Hunter, think about what you're giving up before making any rash decisions over me. Go to Ghana, finish your assignment, and we'll see what happens afterwards.

However, I think we both know you're not going to give up your position and honestly, I don't want you to. Yes, I've fallen in love with you, but I'm willing to let you go."

He chuckled sarcastically. "I'm not changing my mind, woman. I'll see you in four months … maybe less."

"You should go back downstairs to your guests. I'm going to redo my make-up and then check on the bar."

Once he left, she slammed into her desk chair and continued to let the tears fall except this time they weren't so quiet. Harper was afraid of this from the moment they met, and she should've listened to her gut but her heart wanted him. Her time with him had been superb. Passionate. Unforgettable. He was everything she'd ever needed and wanted in a man and more. Now she'd fallen in love with him, but she couldn't let him sacrifice everything for her. Could she?

*****

Sighing, Hunter squeezed Harper's hand when he spotted the international sign along the road at the Atlanta airport. Squeezing his hand back, she placed it on the steering wheel to take a sharp right to veer in the direction to the drop-off area for curbside check-in. She'd been in good spirits for the past few days, helping him pack and cooking home-cooked meals for him. He'd decided not to mention the elephant in the room anymore to ward off any more discussions. He'd meant what he said, and he would be back in four months tops to take the position as director of the US headquarters for Doctors Unlimited.

Harper paralleled parked her two-door Lexus and turned toward him. "This is your stop, sir," she joked, trying to display a smile that turned strained as she leaned her forehead against his. "I'm going to miss the hell out of you, Hunter Arrington."

Cupping her face, he kissed her softy. "I'll be back before you know it."

His chest tightened when he spoke the words. For the first time ever, he wasn't looking forward to his next assignment. For the first time during his career, he finally had a place to call home besides Memphis. It was with Harper and his heart belonged to her.

"Hunter, I mean it when I say, do what's best for you. If you decide to not come back, I'll understand. I've had a wonderful time with you. You're a good man, and I'm glad for the time we've spent together."

"Again, I'll see you soon, beautiful one." He kissed her deeply once more before opening the car door. He scooted around to the trunk that popped when he reached it and began to pull out his two huge rolling suitcases while she grabbed his belongings from the backseat.

"You got it?" she asked, placing his laptop and carry-on bags unto his shoulder and avoiding eye contact as she slid her shades from her hair over her eyes.

"The sun has set, Harp."

Her lips quivered and he let go of the suitcases to yank her to him. "I love you, and I'm going to miss you very much. This will go by fast. I promise. Soon you'll be back here picking me up from the airport."

She laughed. "Go before you miss your flight."

"It doesn't leave for another two almost three hours. I'll be fine."

"Well, the TSA lines in Atlanta are long."

"Are you trying to get rid of me?"

"No, I don't want to prolong our good-bye."

He noted the crack in her tone and said reassuringly, "This isn't good-bye. This is I'll see you soon."

Harper captured his lips in hers and reached deep into his mouth as a frustrated moan released from her. Winding his tongue erratically with hers, the emotions that swept through him tortured his soul and he honestly didn't know how he was going to spend the next four months away from her without going insane.

Reluctantly, Hunter pulled back but didn't let her go. "I love you, beautiful one. I'll call you once I'm settled at the gate."

"Okay, or text me. I have three big celebrity parties tonight simultaneously so I'll be going back and forth checking on them."

"All right."

"Have a safe flight." She slid from his embrace and strolled to her car door. "Call me when you land."

"I will." He gathered his two suitcases and rolled them to the curve. Turning, he watched her zoom away.

Once settled at the gate, he sent Harper a text to let her know he'd made it through the TSA. His phone rang in his hand immediately afterward. He saw Cannon's name, but he'd hoped it was Harper.

"Hey, Cannon. You caught me in time. The ticket agent just announced they're going to begin boarding soon."

"Whew, good. I wanted to inform you that I'm sending Dan and Charles to Ghana as well. They're leaving in the morning."

"Oh, Dan will be there?" Hunter asked somewhat surprised. Their frat brother, Dan, pretty much performed the same job as he did but never together.

"Yeah. Make your job a little easier."

"Well, I appreciate it." His heartbeat raced as a crazy idea popped into his head.

"Maybe you won't have to be there as long and you can go back to Atlanta sooner … unless you've change your mind about taking the position."

"Nah, Cannon. I'm taking it. Truly, for the first time in my career I don't want to go. I thought I'd never say that but meeting Harper has changed my entire life."

"Really? So the two of you decided to call it quits or work it out?"

"We agreed I'd go to Ghana and then if I still felt the same way about her afterward, I'd move back to Atlanta and not continue travelling for Doctors Unlimited. However, I'm not going to change my mind. I love her. I will always love her. Harper is the one, but she keeps saying she doesn't want me to sacrifice my career for her yet she loves me."

"So she's willing to let you go despite that?"

"Something like that. She says it's my true calling and while I've had wonderful experiences, that part is fulfilled. I'm ready to settle in one place … with her."

"Then why are you going?"

Hunter frowned. "Beg your pardon?"

"You heard me. Why are you still in the airport?"

Hunter slowly rose from his seat as a wide smile crossed his face. "Well, it's my job …"

"Dan and Charles can handle it. Are you still going?"

He grabbed his laptop bag and carry-on bag from the chair next to his empty one. "Hell no!"

*****

"How's the bottle service in Unique's area?" Harper asked Shannon as the ladies walked from each VIP section checking on their special guests.

"Perfect. Dawn has it under control."

"Great. Also, check on the party on the rooftop. Josh was having an issue with the ice machine up there, and we may need some back up ice from the machine in the kitchen."

"No problem, Ms. Bennett. Anything else?"

"Yes, make sure to comp out a bottle of Ace of Spades for Briana when she arrives." Harper paused as she opened her Twitter app on her cell phone to check Briana's account. "Make it five for her and her entourage. She always draws a crowd when she tweets where she is, and about five hundred people have shared it in under five minutes and are stating they're coming."

"That's great considering her assistant called an hour ago. I'm going to retweet from the club account and let the security team know."

Harper nodded absentmindedly. While she'd heard the answer, she was numb all over. Everything in front of her was a blur. The loud music seemed to be off in a muted distance as her racing, pounding pulse drowned out Briana's latest number one hit. Since she'd dropped Hunter off, her heart had cracked with each passing second and she had to continue to hold her head high so the tears that needed to spill wouldn't. She couldn't fathom why she hadn't begged him to stay. *Why did I let the only man I've ever been in love with go?*

After Shannon excused herself, Harper trekked over to her favorite spot to watch the crowded dance floor below. Everything was fuzzy and the flashing rainbow lights didn't help matters much either. Spotting a bald head weaving in and out of the dancers, floated her thoughts back to chastising herself over Hunter even more. Drawing her cell phone from the pocket in her flared black skirt, she re-read his text from earlier that she never had a chance to answer.

Made it through TSA. Can't wait to come home to you, beautiful one.

She was truly going to miss him calling her that, but in her heart she knew asking him to sacrifice his career and his love for being hands on with Doctors Unlimited would've been selfish on her part. She was positive that at the end of his assignment in Ghana, he would realize working a nine-to-five wasn't him and he'd go to another country followed by another. That was his life, and she was a detour in the way.

Focusing her stare once more on the scene below, she spotted the bald head again and this time a wave of hysteria and disbelief prickled along her skin. Her next breath wedged deep in her throat as her gaze met his and a cocky grin inched up his face. Shutting her eyes tight, she knew when she opened them he wouldn't be there because it was a mirage. She'd had a shot of whiskey in her office to calm her nerves before heading out to the floor and now it made her imagine Hunter in the club. But he wasn't there. He was flying the friendly skies to Ghana and there was a possibility she'd never see him again.

Taking a deep breath, Harper reopened her eyes and stepped back with a shocked gasp as the hallucination stood directly in front of her.

"Hello, beautiful one."

Her hand flew to her chest to still her rapidly beating heart that had stopped upon dropping him off. "Wa-wait. What are you doing here? You missed your plane?" So many other questions ran rampant through her mind but she couldn't jar them out.

"I didn't miss my plane. I'm not going to Ghana."

"Change of plans?" she whispered, as tremors soared through her body. She reached out to touch his face to make sure he was real. The warmth of his skin under her palm reassured her that he indeed was there.

Taking her hand in his, he slid it to his mouth and kissed it before placing it over his heart. "Yes."

"But ... what about the project?"

"It's being handled. I have a new project."

Her lips quivered as excitement and nervousness crept through her body. She didn't want to get her hopes up but then again she loved him. "Oh, and where's that?" *Please say me!*

"Right here with you, babe."

Her cheeks began to hurt as her wide smile could no longer stretch. "Hunter ... you're here? To stay?"

"Yes, baby. I told you I wasn't giving up on us. I love you, woman."

"And I love you, too. I'm in utter disbelief. Deep down I never wanted you to go but I didn't want to be selfish either."

"Harper, you were willing to sacrifice our relationship because you love me enough to let me go. That signifies you're the woman for me. There's no need for me to go anywhere when everything I want and desire is right here with you. One of the reasons I was always shooting off to the next destination was because I didn't have any responsibilities or ties to hold me down. Yes, I have my family, but not a family or a home of my own. And for once in my life I feel at home with you."

"This is so surreal. I can't believe you're here, but I'm so happy that you are."

"I would've been here sooner, but I needed to meet with your brothers, and I called your parents. They're somewhere in Canada, I believe."

She wrinkled her nose with a light giggle. "Why? You don't need their permission to date me. I'm a grown woman."

"No, but I needed their blessing," he stated, taking her hand and kneeling down to one knee.

"Oh my goodness," she screamed out as the happy tears floated down her cheek. "I can't believe this is happening."

"I love you, beautiful one. I fell for you the second I met you and each moment after that I found myself falling for you even harder. The thought of being without you for four months ... heck, for four hours suffocates my heart more than you could ever imagine. A love like yours is what I've searched for, and now I finally have it and never want to be without you. Will you please do me the honor of being my wife, Harper Elaine Bennett?"

"Yes, yes. A gazillion times yes." Flying into his arms, she smiled as he gathered her up and spun her around before setting her back down. In all of the excitement, she hadn't realized a crowd had gathered around them including her brothers, London, and Simone. Everyone clapped and cheered as Hunter dipped her for a long, amazing kiss.

Epilogue

A year later …

"Baby, this is absolutely gorgeous," Harper stated, gazing out at the tranquil, blue ocean that went on for miles and miles.

Sliding his hands around her waist from behind, Hunter placed a tender kiss to the side of her neck. "I'm glad you're enjoying the yacht, Mrs. Arrington."

"Mmm… I love the way that sounds, Mr. Arrington. And yes, a yacht off the coast of Naples for our honeymoon is the most perfect surprise ever."

"Well, I wanted to do something special for you. You planned a beautiful wedding for us for the past year at The Atlanta Botanical Gardens."

She pivoted in his embrace and encircled her arms around his neck. Resting her bikini top-clad breasts against his bare chest, she sighed as the warmth from the sun touched her back.

"Mmm … yesterday was such a glorious day with all our family and friends, and now this. You sure do know how to spoil me."

"Nothing I wouldn't do for you, beautiful one."

"I know. I realized that the day you didn't go to Ghana. Sometimes I have to pinch myself to believe that all of this is happening. I love you so much, Hunter."

"I love you, too. I knew I had to make you all mine after our first passionate night. I realized then you were everything I wanted in a wife. I'd never felt so at home and comfortable before."

"I do remember the first time we made love. Goodness, you had me thinking that you, too, were the one."

He shook his head as his expression turned serious. "It was a passionate night as well, but actually I'm not referring to that. I mean our first night together. From going with you to Café Intermezzo, to the intense first kiss in the hallway, then watching the basketball game and falling asleep afterwards. Sex isn't the only passionate act. Sometimes being with your soul mate can be fulfilling and romantic. I realized then I wanted many more days and nights like that with you … and of course making love to you is definitely a perk."

"Yes, it is. I have to say last night's escapade was highly intense."

He yanked her all the way against him. "We can do it again tonight."

"Looking forward to it for the next two weeks and for the rest of our lives."

Picking her up, he sat down with her on a chaise lounge and pulled her close to him. "I still can't believe you've changed your schedule at the club. Only three nights a week? Are you sure you can handle being away from the club?"

"Yes, because I can't handle being away from you. Besides, my brothers understand that I'm married now and I want to be home when you get off work whenever possible. I've worked at Masquerade since straight out of college. Plus, some of what I do can be done during the day and my staff is awesome."

"Thank you. I look forward to having you to myself on some evenings now."

"Besides, you made a big sacrifice for me. And when we start having babies, I may even take off for a year or so. That's what my mother did."

"Well, she did have triplets," Hunter said with a smirk.

"Yep, and you're a twin sooooo …"

"Hmm, you think we may have multiples, as well?"

"I hope so. That would be cool. I love my brothers very much and we're so close. It would be wonderful for our children. However, it doesn't matter. I just want healthy, happy babies with you."

"When do you want to start?" he asked with a raised eyebrow.

"How about on our next anniversary, and we'll spend this year practicing."

Flipping her over on the chaise, he slid his body on top of hers.

"I take it you want to *practice* right now, Mr. Arrington?"

"Yes, beautiful one. Right now."

The End

The Bennett Triplets Series

But that's not the end. In case you didn't know, there are two more novellas in the series that are available and written by my fabulous friends. Check out the blurbs below.

*****

A Passionate Love by Delaney Diamond

Simone Brooks and Cameron Bennett should not be together. She's a wealthy socialite looking for a suitable husband. A man with the right pedigree and an economic status that matches her own. He's part owner of the hottest nightclub in Atlanta with his siblings. Someone who loves cooking, the outdoors, and women, not necessarily in that order.

After one night together, their sizzling chemistry makes it difficult to stay away. Then comes the hard part—navigating their differences to salvage a relationship that, while it may be imperfect, overflows with love and passion.

*****

A Passionate Kiss by Sharon C. Cooper

Retired Marine, Mason Bennett, has two goals: adjust to civilian life and keep drama out of it. His focus is on his role as part-owner, along with his siblings, of Atlanta's hottest nightclub. However, his attention shifts when the woman he has loved like a sister reenters his life and thoughts of a passionate kiss they shared hijacks his mind. Their connection is explosive. Feelings he's tried to deny come to the forefront, and he's tempted to do something he thought he would never do—cross that line from friends to lovers.

TV news anchor, London Alexander, is back home in Atlanta and ready to start a new chapter in her life. This time she hopes her future includes Mason, the man she has loved forever. She's ready to step over the forbidden line that he's drawn in their relationship.

Will taking a chance on love lead to a happily-ever-after? Or will risking their friendship leave them both with broken hearts?

ABOUT THE AUTHOR

Candace Shaw writes romance novels because she believes that happily-ever-after isn't found only in fairy tales. When she's not writing or researching information for a book, you can find Candace in her gardens, shopping, reading or learning how to cook a new dish.

Candace lives in Atlanta, Georgia with her loving husband and their loyal dog, Ali. She is currently working on her next fun, flirty and sexy romance.

You can contact Candace on her website at www.CandaceShaw.net, on Facebook at https://www.facebook.com/AuthorCandaceShaw or tweet her at https://twitter.com/Candace_Shaw.

Books by Candace Shaw

The Arrington Family Series

Cooking up Love
The Game of Seduction
Only One for Me
Prescription for Desire
My Kind of Girl

Chasing Love Series (Harlequin Kimani Romance)

Her Perfect Candidate
Journey to Seduction
The Sweetest Kiss
His Loving Caress
A Chase for Christmas (December 2016)

Precious Moments Series

For the Love of You
When I Fell for You (Winter 2016)
Then There was You (Late Spring 2017)

Free Reads

Simply Amazing (Arrington Family Series)
Only You for Christmas (Chasing Love/Harlequin's
website only)

CPSIA information can be obtained
at www.ICGtesting.com
Printed in the USA
BVHW030214190521
607700BV00005B/13

9 781537 082332